Some From Zacatecas

Tamar Diana Wilson

Plain View Press
P. O. 42255
Austin, TX 78704

plainviewpress.net
pk@plainviewpress.net
512-441-2452

ISBN: 978-1-935514-36-7
Library of Congress Number: 2010922429

Cover art by Natasha Mayers
Cover design by Susan Bright

Acknowledgements

Although I could not have written this book without knowing people I met in Los Angeles and Mexcali and learning of their experiences, this is a work of fiction.

Earlier versions of "From L.A. to New York. . . ." and "The Crossing" were published in *Struggle*.

Contents

1981-1984

One: **Maíz**

August, 1981

Mundo stood in the midst of dried-out dusty corn stalks. The bean
vines wound around the stalks were fading into yellow as well. The
squash, just like the ears of corn, were half their normal size, and many
had been invaded by ants and flies. The smell of green was gone. The
intermittent buzzing of insects, the occasional caw of a crow and the
swishing tail of the tethered mule broke the silence. A buzzard circled
up above the *monte*, then suddenly descended.

Mundo looked up at the pale blue sky bereft of even the tiniest
cumulus. He removed his *tejana* and wiped the sweat from his forehead,
then ran his fingers through the mass of straight black hair, unruly
hair which tumbled over his eyes and fell onto his rounded child-like
cheeks in an otherwise square face. He replaced his *tejana* and tugged
at his red-black mustache, as he often did when worried or unsure of
himself. Antonio said to come if the harvest failed again, he thought.
Antonio was his older brother, who had crossed the border two years
ago, when his two hectares had been flooded out and the corn and
beans and squash destroyed. *Ay cabrón*, the *rancho* where they lived,
the region, was always hit by too much water or too little, like a curse,
Mundo reflected. Driving us all out to *el otro lado*, the other side.

Mundo walked along a furrow, between the musty chalk-like corn
stalks, his boots kicking up the earth turned to khaki dust. His cousin
Nicolás had left with their uncle Ignacio only about a week ago.
Ignacio would cross for the seventh time, Nicolás for the first. Nicolás
had no land, being a middle son, and with the failed harvest there was
no work for him even on the nearby hacienda. Nicolás had not had
much luck when he farmed his brother's lands the year before, when
the harvest was good enough for almost everyone else to get along.

Nicolás hated leaving his wife, Mundo knew, as much as Mundo
hated leaving his Petra and his week old son Benjamin. But there were
medical bills to worry about. Big medical bills for a poor *campesino*,
a poor farmer. Because the midwife had said she couldn't deal with
an opening as small as Petra's, that she could not guarantee a live
birth, that Petra could even die. So when the pains came, Mundo
paid Don Rigoberto, the best off of those who lived on the *rancho*

9

because of his days as a bracero, to take him and his mother and Petra in Don Rigoberto's pick-up, squeaking and groaning all the way, to the clinic in Fresnillo. It took Petra twenty-six hours to give birth. The doctor wanted to open her up and take the baby out, but Petra refused, knowing how much more money that would cost, saying that she wanted her child born naturally. While Mundo and his mother waited, they cursed their poverty, "Why must we be so poor that my grandchild, your child risks death?" his mother asked, twisting her handkerchief in her hands.

At her suggestion Mundo had made a *manda* to the *Niño de Atocha*, "*Santo Niño*, if you let my son live I will let his hair grow long and not cut it for three years. Then I will bring him to you and we will dedicate his hair to you in your church in Plateritos." Benjamin was finally born, red-faced, and crying lustily, his little head adorned by centimeters of straight black hair. And Petra, worn and slender, slender as the stalks of corn, the bulge now gone from her belly, was all right too. It seemed that the *Niño de Atocha* had heard his promise.

Mundo reached out and pulled at a leaf on the corn stalk. It crumbled in his hands, left only a web of rough strings. The drought stricken harvest would scarcely suffice to meet the corn needs of his mother and father and sister and brother this year, much less for his and Petra's. And there would be nothing left over to sell, to buy matches and lard and salt and other things they needed. Except perhaps for the tiny wage his father earned caring for cows on the hacienda. *Ay cabrón*, where would the cash come from to pay the medical bills? There was nothing to sell. Except the land itself. Or the two cows that gave them milk. Then they would have nothing for next year. "Never give up your land," his father had told him. "Your grandfather, my father, died in the Revolution so we could have land. A million *mexicanos* died so that we could have land. Without land one must leave the *campo* and beg for work in the big cities, where there are thousands even millions of people who do not know you, who will not give you a helping hand. Without land, there is nothing to pass on to even one son. Always remember, our land is our refuge."

Antonio had told him to come. Antonio had said there were jobs that paid more a day that you earned a week in Fresnillo. That the only problem was the crossing, that he should cross with a buddy, not try it alone.

Mundo looked up at the sky again. Not the slightest wisp or whiff of cloud. His cousin Luís, Nicolás's older brother, had come back to the *rancho* two weeks ago. Luís was so long absent from the *rancho* that he had lent his two hectares to Nicolás to farm. But Nicolás didn't have enough money or even one cow to provide fertilizer, and he wasn't much of a farmer in any case, he was better at harvesting than sowing. So Luís gave it to Don Rigoberto to sharecrop. But this year not even Don Rigoberto could get enough out of it for half the harvest to feed Luís's wife and brood. They would have to buy corn for tortillas somewhere else.

Mundo considered that he might be able to cross with Luís. Luís planned to leave in another day or two. Perhaps he could even earn enough money in *el norte* to pay the doctor's bills and send money to Petra for food and perhaps a new dress or two, and maybe even enough money so they could build their own room beside his father's house.

Mundo tugged at his red-black moustache, looked at the pale blue sky one last time, mounted his mule, and headed back to the windowless two room adobe house where he lived with his mother and father, his sister Gabriela, his little brother, his wife Petra, and now his son, Benjamin. He would tell them tonight that he was going.

Two: **The Crossing**

September, 1981

"What damned bad luck," Luís observed. "We were held up for almost twelve hours."

"And bad luck comes in threes," Mundo repeated the old adage. "Who knows what awaits us in Tecate. Or crossing the border."

"They kept my gold chain with the horse. The one Sara gave me. I forgot to ask for it back," Luís said as he fingered the neckline of his pearl-buttoned western shirt.

It had been a beautiful gold chain, twisted links pressing into one another, and it held a galloping golden horse. Sara had given it to him two years before, on the occasion of their first anniversary. Sara was his mistress in the United States, a young woman who had escaped the violence in El Salvador to work first in a garment factory and later in a restaurant in Los Angeles. Small, with curly auburn hair, she had been at a rodeo dance in El Monte when first he met her. She had worked hard to buy him that golden chain and horse, symbol of their union in lieu of a wedding ring.

In any case, he was married to someone else. To his Laura. Married for eleven years and with five children. A new one conceived almost every time he went back to Santa Martha. He had married a girl from a nearby *rancho* when he was twenty. Slender and with lovely long chestnut hair, she was the first *novia* he had ever had. But he was so lonely in the United States, where he had been most of the time for the past six years, returning only every two years to his *rancho* for scarcely a month at a time, that when he met Sara he had grasped onto her as a way of easing the loneliness.

O

From Fresnillo, Zacatecas they took the bus to Guadalajara and from Guadalajara they changed buses to Mexicali. From there they would go to Tecate. Between Guadalajara, Jalisco and Mexicali, Baja California there were many customs and immigration checkpoints, even for those traveling north. Two young men in shabby, baggy pants and t-shirts from a second-hand clothing stall and dusty baseball caps had boarded the bus on the other side of Tepic, Nayarit, having waved down the bus as it made its way north. They carried small backpacks that they placed in the luggage container several rows away from where they sat. When the *federales* boarded the bus in Hermosillo, Sonora, they did a routine check of the luggage. The backpacks were not claimed by any of the passengers and when opened for inspection revealed 10 kilos of marijuana in each. The passengers without luggage were marched into the guard house: the two from outside Tepic, Luís and Mundo, and two others heading for the border.

They were held for twelve hours inside, while the driver was not permitted to move the bus until the carriers were found. The guards applied stomach punches and cattle prods to all six, to see who would admit that the backpacks were theirs. The boys in the baseball caps held out for that long before confessing. The *federales* had confiscated all valuables, including wallets, identification cards, and jewelry before the questioning began. When released, Luís had been so happy to be free that he remembered only to collect his wallet. He forgot to ask for his chain and horse, which he never took off, even when showering.

"Are these your backpacks," the short, heavy set, balding *federale* had asked Luís. "No official, he had replied.

A stomach punch beating the air out of his stomach and lungs had been the response. "Then where is your luggage, *pendejo*"

"We have none. My cousin and I are just going to visit my sister in Tecate. We have clothes there." Luís was lying, but not about having no luggage. He and Mundo had none. He did not want to reveal that the planned to cross the border without documents. The *federales* were capable of sending them back the twenty-six hours to Zacatecas. They would lose weeks from their journey before they would be able to put together a loan to finance their bus fare back to Tecate, Baja California again. Don Lucas charged ten percent interest a month. It would have to be someone else, someone returning from Los Angeles or Chicago who was bringing money to their families.

○

They arrived tired and covered with dust that filtered hazily through the open windows of the old bus. They de-boarded outside the small bus station, and walked into the waiting room. The room was filled with men in journey worn clothes, trying to sleep in the worn red plastic chairs or on the floor. "It's good we have money to stay in the hotel. At least I remembered to get my wallet back," Luís observed.

They exited the waiting room and walked the three blocks to the Hotel del Norte, where it was only five dollars per night per person, as many to the room as could be housed together.

Luís met the manager smoking a *delicado* in the mottled green lobby. "Got a room?" he asked. Mundo looked around him, noting every fly on the wall, every slowly turning ceiling fan. He had never been in a hotel before. He had never been farther than Fresnillo, two hours by bus from his *rancho* before, except to visit the *Niño de Atocha* after his son was born. That had been a three hour walk from Fresnillo.

"Not unless you want to share and they want to share with you," the manager answered.

At that moment Nicolás, Luís's younger brother, stuck his head out a door down the hallway. "You finally fucking got here," he yelled to Luís and Mundo. "*Que padre!*"

"What are you still doing here," Mundo demanded. "You left the *rancho* more than a week ago!" Luís carefully took a ten dollar bill out of his wallet and handed it to the manager. Mundo and Luís moved toward the room where Nicolás was standing in the doorway.

"We tried to cross three times and had to turn back each time," Nicolás answered, opening the door wider so they could pass through to the fly speckled grey room with three cots and a brown stained sink.

"Hi there, boys," their uncle Ignacio waved to them from the cot farthest from the door. He and Nicolás had come to Tecate to cross together. Only a fool would try to cross without a *compañero*. And it was Nicolás's first time. Mundo's too.

Luís and Nicolás shook hands with the other two dark, wrinkled men who were sharing the room. From Durango, they had been part of the group that the coyote contracted by Nicolás and Ignacio had formed, and unsuccessfully, tried to cross.

O

It was after 8 p.m. the following day that the *coyote* came for them. Besides Ignacio, Nicolás, Luís and Mundo and the two men from Durango a couple with a baby was in their group. Ignacio grumbled about it a bit because with a woman and a baby they would have to move over the hills more slowly.

They had assembled at the cast iron fence by 9 and with the *coyote* and his helper pushing them on they went over it one by one. The father carried the child, peacefully sleeping, strapped to his back.

Then the climb onto the rock-strewn hills began. Larger rocks than they had ever seen, and small boulders close together so that it was hard to find a passageway, a foothold on the ground. The woman, Ignacio and Nicolás had worn tennis shoes and had an easier time of it than the men in their western boots. At one point the sole came away from one of Mundo's aged dusty boots. He tied it together with his handkerchief and kept going. Mundo decided that if he ever crossed again he would wear tennis shoes as well.

Suddenly they heard footsteps, many of them, on the rocky clusters over to their right. The *coyote* motioned for them to stop and remain quiet. It might have been the border patrol, though with their infrared telescopes mounted on pick-ups and jeeps, they seldom got out to scout around. Only if they had spotted them. Eventually they saw in the distance another group of eight making their way over a nearby crest. The *coyote* motioned them to keep going. He had explained earlier that they were going to a point on route 8 then would drive to the north on route 5. Although this meant something to Ignacio and Luís it meant nothing to Nicolás and Mundo. "Route 8 goes toward the coast," Luís explained. "Then route 5 goes north to Los Angeles."

The *coyote* would let them off before reaching San Clemente, then post his helper as a lookout to see when they closed down the migration checkpoint. They would have to wait in the surrounding hills, until he gave them the signal that all was clear.

Foot-weary, sweating, and anxious they finally made it to the white paneled truck parked in a rest stop. Luís, thinking of his own children, had carried the child for a part of the way, putting the harness on his own back. "*Gracías, amigo*," the father had said.

After they entered the truck the *coyote* and his helper loaded several rows of used tires, pushed in after them. Then they headed off west on route 8 and all was well until they passed Pinesdale. The baby was crying softly in the back of the truck. "Shut it up," the *coyote* ordered as the slowed for the border patrol jeep and were waved down.

An immigration official came over to the truck, driven by the *coyote's* helper.

"Where are you coming from?" was his first question.

"Yuma, Arizona," the helper answered in almost unaccented English. The immigration officer flashed his flashlight on the plates. Arizona plates.

"Where are you going?"

"San Diego," was the reply.

"What's your business there?"

"We're delivering a load of used tires."

"To who?"

"To Lucky's Automobiles. A used car place."

"At three o'clock in the morning?"

"They open at six. We plan on having breakfast at McDonalds."

"For three hours? Open up and let's see what you have."

The *coyote* hopped out and opened the back of the truck. The immigration officer moved one of the tires to see what was behind it. More tires.

"O.K., Get going."

Meanwhile, all ten adults in the back of the truck had kept as silent as possible. The mother of the crying baby had placed her hand over his mouth so that he could emit no sounds that might cause them to be discovered. It was not until the truck began moving again that she took her hand away. The baby didn't cry. Didn't move toward her breast as he usually did. She shook him. There was no response. She handed the baby to her husband, sitting close beside her, an alarmed look on her face. He reached for the child, patted him on the back, holding him close to his shoulder. The baby did not move. The baby's face was red, almost purple, the eyes bulging. But the blood was going slowly out of his inflated cheeks. The baby became paler and paler, his limbs stiffened. The mother grabbed her child and began to wail, loudly, uncontrollably. Wailing like a police siren following them in the night.

○

They were in the safe house in El Monte by 7:30 a.m. The otherwise successful journey had been marred by the dead baby and his distraught parents. There were six others there, four men and two women, each sitting on the floor with back against the wall—waiting. Waiting for someone, relative or friend, to pay their crossing fees to the *coyote* and come to pick them up.

Ignacio and Luís had left their three hundred dollars each with
Antonio before they went back to Mexico. Antonio would have
to borrow to pay for Mundo and Nicolás though. He was their only
relative. And they would pay him back after they found jobs.

The problem was that Antonio had already left for work by the time
they got to the safe house. The *coyote* wouldn't be able to call him until
after six that evening. And they hadn't eaten since prior to crossing the
border. It could be worse, sometimes crossings took up to three days,
Ignacio told them. They had been lucky that the checkpoint in San
Clemente had been closed at the time they arrived. Sometimes you hid
in the fields outside San Clemente for twenty-four hours or more and
only if you had money would the *coyote* go to get you food—usually
something like crackers or cookies and a soda.

Antonio knew they were coming of course. Ignacio had called him
collect, the night they planned to leave Tecate the first time. And the
coyote, of course, had called as well, to make sure he had the money.
But whether the crossing would be successful was an unknown. Ignacio
and Nicolás had failed the first three attempts. That Mundo and
Luís had crossed so quickly left Antonio little time to get the money
together for his brother Mundo.

The four of them found a wall space and leaned back against the
dirty grey wall to sleep.

They woke about 11 a.m. and were hungry. Ignacio asked one of
the women associated with the *coyote* if there was food and would
she sell it to them. "Beans and tortillas," she replied. "Five dollars a
plate." Luckily Ignacio had brought thirty dollars with him. He paid
for the four of them, then ordered two plates for the mother and father
of the dead baby, buried somewhere near San Clemente, while they
waited for the *coyote* to return and tell them when they could pass the
checkpoint.

◯

The woman, whose name they knew was Martha, had cried and
protested that she wanted the baby to be blessed by a priest before they
buried her. "Martha, *mi* Martha," her husband cried, holding her close,
"We must bury him here. I'll make a cross of stone. But we do not
know how long it will be to Los Angeles. Or how long it will be until
your aunt can come for us." Helplessly, the woman released her grip

on the small body, hugged closely to her breast, and her husband took the dead baby from her. He drug a trench, helped by Luís and one of the men from Durango, and the other men looked for rocks to make a small cross.

Mundo, thinking of his small son, offered a prayer, "May the soul of this little one join the angels in heaven and never fear hunger or cold or suffering again."

As each of them began to throw a handful of earth over the baby's inert body in its shallow grave, the child's mother became hysterical, shouting "I killed my baby. I killed my baby." She moved toward the small grave, tried to pull out the body her child. Her husband moved toward her, gathered her in his arms and forced her to stop her flailing.

"There is nothing to be done," he said.

"Cursed land," she replied.

Her husband thanked Mundo for his heartfelt prayer. He held his wife closely in his arms and murmured to her that she must accept their destiny, that they would have other children, that the baby now would not suffer anymore but become an *angelito*. Tears streamed down both their faces. And the seven men and one woman sat waiting in a field outside of San Clemente until another truck came to pick them up.

The woman barely touched her beans, brought in the smallest soup bowls any of them had ever seen. Her husband ate, slowly, and as though it were a necessary task he was performing, and wiped his mouth with a tortilla after finishing his meal. After eating, the four men from Zacatecas talked among themselves, quietly. They avoided talking about the dead baby, glimpsing occasionally at the child's parents who sat stunned by life, victims of a false hope. But they only glimpsed, not wishing to meet their eyes and read the pain contained in them. And they tried to talk of happy things.

Luís told Mundo and Nicolás about the rodeo in El Monte, exactly like the rodeos in Zacatecas and followed by a dance. The problem was getting someone with a car who wanted to drive out—it was almost an hour if you took streets, from the apartment in Santa Monica. But you could go to Santa Monica pier and play electronic games, and that was only fifteen, twenty minutes away by bus. Nicolás and Mundo did not know what electronic games were, and even though Luís tried to explain PacMan, a mouth running through a maze eating up small figures, they just looked at him as though he were talking about another planet, and he gave up. You'll just have to see, he said. But when you go wear a baseball cap not a *tejana*, and they'll think you're a Chicano and not a Mexican, he advised them.

As six p.m. approached Luís advised the *coyote's* helper that Antonio would be home, could he call. The found out that Antonio hadn't been able to borrow a car, or find someone to come for them. "It's twenty-five dollars a head more if we bring them to Santa Monica," the *coyote* had told him. It seemed that Antonio had the money to pay for Mundo and Miguel. And he had agreed to pay the hundred dollars more as well, if they came after eight p.m.

○

It was only a few hours after they arrived in the apartment Antonio was sharing with Ignacio and his wife's brother Edgar that Mundo broke down. "A baby boy," he told Antonio, tears streaming silently down his face. "It could have been my son. My Benjamin."

Nicolás stifled a sob. He had two baby girls at home. "I didn't know crossing could be so hard on people," he said.

Luís commented, "They must have been from El Salvador. They were so afraid of being deported."

Nicolás spoke. "She didn't put her hand over the baby's nose. I don't think so anyway. Just over his mouth. The baby had mucus in his nose. He had a cold. That's why he smothered. No mother would kill her baby. Not even if they were from El Salvador. She couldn't have put her hand over the baby's nose and mouth at the same time. It just happened. The baby had a cold. He couldn't breathe. The *señora* just tried to keep her baby from crying. Just covered up his mouth."

Mundo looked at Nicolás and Luís, then said, in a longer passage that anyone had ever heard him say, "I don't remember the details. The *señora* was just trying to keep the baby quiet. So they wouldn't be caught and sent back. So we wouldn't get caught and sent back. They must have been from El Salvador because it wouldn't have been such a big thing to be sent back to Mexico and cross again another day. But in El Salvador it is a *desmadre* a fucked up mess. I saw about it on the news one night at Don Roberto's house. People killing people in the street. Even kids with great big guns, maybe machine guns."

"They must have been afraid to go back. Return from there all over again, all the way through all of Mexico," Ignacio observed.

"So why not say they are from Mexico?" Antonio asked. If they were deported back to El Salvador the baby might have died there. The whole family. They should just say they are Mexicans." He paused and looked for confirmation.

"*Puede ser*," said Ignacio. "Could be."

Luís nodded. "Some of Sara's friends are learning about who is governor of the state they are going to say they are from and who is president of Mexico and who was president before. And stuff like that the immigration asks some of them who try to say they are Mexicans but are from Guatemala and El Salvador. There is even an organization downtown that teaches them to pass themselves off as Mexicans. So they are not sent all the way back. Thousands of miles back. Three times from Zacatecas back."

Antonio looked down at the toes of his boots. Tried to change the subject from the baby. They all had babies. It was too close to home. "Once we lost a *viejo* on a crossing. Remember the time we crossed together Luís? He was bit by a snake. He didn't make it to the safe house before he died. Heart failure they said."

"Was it a rattler?" Mundo asked.

"Don't know. We didn't see it. Didn't hear it either, like you would if it had been a rattler. Just saw a body slithering away in the moonlight," Antonio replied.

Edgar didn't say much, as usual. Just looked down at the rug between his outstretched knees, hands folded, light brown hair falling over his forehead. When he had crossed with Antonio just a year ago they had been caught and deported after a fourteen-hour stay in the Border Patrol compound at Brownsville air base. No one had given them food in all that time. From Tijuana they made their way back to Tecate, to the *coyote* they knew, and crossed successfully on the next try. But he hadn't seen anyone die on the way.

A lump in his throat, Edgar wondered that once he married Antonio's sister Gabriela, how he would get her across. She must come to join him. He knew he would spend the rest of his working life in the United States. He had no land on the *rancho*, it had all gone to pay the doctor bills for his father's many heart attacks. He would have to support his widowed mother and younger brother with the wages he earned in the United States, until his younger brother turned 16 and his mother let him cross as well. That would be two years from now.

It was almost a year now since he had seen Gabriela, shy, plump, sweet girl whom he had promised himself to return to marry. Neither he nor she knew how to read or write, so they had no contact. He had had to help in the fields too young, she had problems with her eyes and her family couldn't afford glasses for her. So they hadn't gone to school, even the two years offered on the *rancho*. He was shy about speaking to her on the telephone at Don Roberto's house, and had no right to do so, since they were not yet official *novios*. He had not yet officially asked her father for permission to marry. He had not had the money for the liquor and presents that had to be given on such an occasion. He would do so when he returned.

Edgar did not mention his love for Gabriela to her brothers. They must have known, having seen him in front of their house, talking to her in low tones, grasping her hands, sometimes being invited inside for a tortilla and beans. There were no secrets on the *rancho*. No private places to go. Except up into the hills, the *monte*. But a man did not take a woman there, a woman he wanted to marry. Though there were rumors that Antonio had taken Lucha there before they were married. Lucha had gone there to pick *nopales* and prickly pear several times. But never alone. She always took their younger brother, Rogelio.

If only Lucha, his sister, were here, she would help him send a letter. When his father got sick with the heart trouble, their mother had sent her to live with their Aunt Lidia, in a *pueblo* and hour away, and Lucha had finished primary school there. But then Gabriela would have to find someone to read it for her—maybe her sister Lucy who had gone to school for two years, the only schooling they offered on their *rancho*. Though for some reason Edgar didn't totally trust Lucy to remain silent.

In another year he would return, when he had enough money to pay for their wedding. He wanted her, a middle child who had received little affection, to have her wedding in white. He had hoped originally to return in just one year, but he hadn't found steady work at first, just loading trucks now and then, sometimes painting or gardening or cleaning up a property two or three days a week.

Now he had a job cleaning offices on Pico Boulevard, with his aunt's husband who lived in Inglewood. It was night work, which he didn't like so much, but it was steady work, six nights a week with Saturday off, and it paid the minimum wage—which some of the short-term jobs he had had did not.

Yes, soon he would marry, one year more. And bring Gabriela across, some safer way than climbing over the rock-strewn mountains outside of Tecate. Before they had a baby who might die on the crossing.

Three: **Sawtelle Boulevard I (1981-1992)**

Sawtelle Boulevard 6 a.m.
Begins to fill with numbers of men
dressed in Goodwill or Salvation Army clothing,
from Guatemala, El Salvador, mostly Mexico:
By seven there are at least ten
clustered on each and every corner
and in front of every store
from the seven eleven on Santa Monica
to *loncheras* parked along the street,
past Olympic, down to Pico
some with cousins or brothers who share their plight,
some with just one friend:
All looking for employment,
Whatever may come their way.

A number are selected for a few hours work
by the neighborhood's Japanese nurseries
lining Sawtelle Boulevard.
Trucks filled with gardening tools stand by
to load up some laborers
before continuing on to Beverly Hills
where aunts and nieces work as maids.
Construction cleanup is sometimes offered
or loading and unloading of semi-trailer trucks,
for sweatshops where sweethearts and sisters may be employed,
for less than minimum wage.
They take whatever comes their way,
Not asking how much they will be paid.

They live from five to twenty or even more
in apartments from Sepulveda to eleventh,
from West L.A. to Santa Monica, even Venice
sending all they can to widowed mothers, wives and children
if they've been left behind, as probably they were,
(it costs less if you come alone)
on some small rural *rancho* where tourists do not visit

or in some semi-serviced squatter settlement also off limits
where floors are of earth, and the rain leaks in:
It is perhaps where they'd rather be,
at home in Mexico, Guatemala or El Salvador:
But they take whatever comes their way
So their families can survive.

Four: **Sawtelle Boulevard II**

One day after arriving in Los Angeles Mundo and Nicolás, led by
Ignacio, turned east on Santa Monica Boulevard at Bundy, and headed
toward Sawtelle, more than a mile away. Ramon Ayala's *"Bonita Finca
de Adobe"* emanated from the small store near the corner even at this
early hour, the front windows adorned with cassetts by Los Invasores
de Nuevo León, Los Tigres del Norte and Los Bukis, among other
groups from Mexico. The melody followed them almost a block before
being erased by the sounds of traffic, the roar of a muffler, the squeak of
brakes, the ragged sound of rubber tires rubbing on tarmac. The cool
breeze of early morning caressed their unshaven faces, stiff prickles of
beards ignored since yesterday. They passed an immense grocery store
with a "Safeway" sign mounted near the top of its red-painted façade,
perhaps the grocery store where Antonio had promised to take them,
Mundo thought, overwhelmed by its size, the immense parking lot
dotted by dribbles and drops of motor oil and an occasional sparrow
pecking at something then fleeing to the nearby avocado trees. They
walked on by the block long complex labeled "Ford Company" exuding
smells of engine parts and lubricants, followed by the aroma of fried
eggs and bacon from the diner across the street, lasting only seconds
before being overpowered by exhaust fumes from myriad cars headed
east and headed west. *Cabrón*, I never knew there were so many cars in
this world, and such pretty ones, thought Mundo.

They walked fast, not talking, the soles of Mundo's bandaged boots
heated up, the nails almost pushing through the newspaper filling
burned once again against his heel. They passed a carwash, heard
Spanish spoken by short dark men with rags in hand who reminded
them of Mexico. His fists in the pockets of the jacket Antonio had
lent him, Mundo felt with his thumbs the soft balls of lint, and hard
little dots of tobacco fell from the cigarettes Antonio had sometimes
sequestered there one by one, in his attempt to smoke fewer every day.
They walked by a book store whose windows were filled by more books
than Mundo had ever seen in one place, all different, and Mundo
wondered what anyone did with so many books, he who had to spell
out each word just to read a newspaper. The trio passed the coffee
shop with its bitter sweet aroma combined with the sugar-smell of
newly baked jelly doughnuts and arrived almost immediately at their
destination.

Ignacio seldom talked unless he felt it was absolutely necessary. But he was their guide today. Ignacio pointed out the Goodwill second hand store to their left: "You can buy work clothes there. And shoes. And pots and pans and dishes if you ever need more."

They turned right, going south on Sawtelle, past small groups in twos and threes and fours of men from Mexico, Guatemala and El Salvador, past a small store selling sodas, tamales and canned goods, past a number of nurseries side by side, where the scent of bougainvillea, roses and daffodils combined with the bitter of narcissus and the tang of lemon tree blossoms. They are owned by *japoneses*" Ignacio pointed out. "Sometimes they give us work. But you must come early. Eight o'clock is not early enough. But now you know where to come to look for jobs. This is the street."

"Best time six or seven?" asked Mundo.

"Yeah, for landscaping. Or loading and unloading trucks," Ignacio answered.

The three men stopped on the south side of the last nursery. Mundo took a hand from the pockets of Antonio's jacket, tugged as his moustache and flashed a smile, "That's the best jobs for country boys like us?"

"Or construction clean-up work," Ignacio replied. "For short time jobs. That's what I like. A few weeks here, a few days there. It doesn't get boring that way."

"And for long term?" Nicolás asked, even though he was inclined to Ignacio' way of thinking.

"Well there's factory work. But I hear they close you in for ten hours a day, six days a week, and not a window to let the sunshine in. Then they are at least an hour away by bus, down in downtown." Ignacio paused, rubbed his chin with a calloused hand. "The best is to get steady gardening jobs like Antonio and Luís have."

As they talked they saw vans and pick-ups, but only a few, pass and stop by one group of men or other, sticking one or two or three fingers out of the driver's side window. Men rushed over. The driver pointed to the ones he wanted and they climbed in.

"That's how they will call you to work," Ignacio said. "But I just want you to get the feel of things today. Most at this hour want someone to paint their houses, inside or out or both. Or move furniture."

"Well, let's go today," Nicolás and Mundo said almost in unison.

"O.K. then boys. Let's try to go together. Watch for three fingers and then run for it."

○

"Everything is so new here," thought Mundo as they waited. "Supermarkets as big as Conasupo corn storage warehouses. Expanses of cement road and sidewalk without potholes. Gleaming cars. And numerous jobs, numerous ways to earn money. Soon I'll be able to pay the doctor in Fresnillo for helping my wife give me Benjamin," he thought. "And then return to my brother Antonio the money for the *coyote*. And then," he speculated, "I can send money so Petra can put up a separate room for us. And maybe buy another cow"

○

Things did not turn out so easy. They only got a day's work moving furniture and two day's work replanting a garden the first week. Most of the first day's wages Mundo spent at the Goodwill on some green gabardine pants, two grey sweatshirts, a faded blue baseball cap like the one his uncle Ignacio wore, and wrinkled but comfortable brown work boots. He was amazed at the number of racks of dresses and decided to come back before he returned to the *rancho* and buy a bunch of them for Petra, his mother, and his sisters. Part of the first day's wages also went to pay part of his portion of the grocery bill. He was able to give his second day's wages of $40 to Antonio for the $300 he owed him for bringing him across. And Antonio took it to whoever he had borrowed it from, as he did Nicolás's contribution. Ignacio had left money behind to pay for his re-crossing and was flush enough to bring them home a dozen sugared jelly doughnuts—which neither Nicolás or Mundo had ever tasted before. The next week Nicolás put away money to buy a jelly doughnut every morning that they walked by the coffee shop near Sawtelle. Mundo, on the other hand, saved every penny he could.

○

Mundo got lucky though, a couple of weeks later. Antonio had been working with his *compadre* Alvaro, from a neighboring *rancho*, less than two miles from their own Santa Marta. Alvaro had crossed the border almost twenty years before, going to Salinas to work first in the lettuce fields, then in a packaging plant. His wife Rosario came after him when rumors got back to the *rancho* that he had begun an affair with one of the women workers. She had a cousin in Los Angeles and convinced Alvaro to move down there. They took a room in the old motel converted into one-room apartments called "Cozy Corners" on Sawtelle below Olympic, where her uncle and his family also lived. It was where the workers ran for cover, given protection by anyone who lived there, when *la migra* came. There was a law that *la migra* couldn't enter private homes, and all those on the street soon learned this.

Alvaro and Rosario were thinking of going back to Salinas now. There was work in the fields and in the packaging plants for both of them and for their teenage sons and daughter, all born back on Rosario's *rancho*—she had not wanted to give birth in the United States. So, there was a job opening for Mundo with Antonio, in the same complex on the hill overlooking the San Fernando Valley, with its row houses and private homes, a gated community where Luís had also once worked before moving in with Sara. They were picked up each morning by the foreman, a slender middle-aged man with a sad look in his eyes from the other side of Jeréz in Zacatecas who drove an old Ford of painted and repainted multiple colors of brown and tan, the trunk filled with gardening tools.

And sometimes Antonio talked of getting his own gardening route, if only he could get enough money together to buy a pick-up.

Five: **Lucha Letter**

Rancho Santa Martha
January, 1983

Antonio, my beloved husband,

May this letter find you well as this is my desire. I write to tell you that I have begun the second room of our little house. With the money you sent me I bought adobes from Don Rigoberto's son and one wall is up already now and I use it as a washing room. I got them cheaply because my little brother Rogelio is working for him now and learning to make adobes and bricks. Miguelito and I live quite comfortably in the first room but as always we miss you and wish you were here with us or us there with you. Sometimes we still stay with your mother so that it is less lonely and of course we still eat with her, and I help her making tortillas and cleaning the beans and washing the clothes and I am writing to ask permission if I can buy a stove with the next money you send me and my mother has an extra gas tank that she will lend me. Then when you come I can cook dinner for your in our own little house and I miss you terribly and when I go up to the monte to pick nopales with my little brother I remember the times we went there together. I have told you that many times before and maybe you will think me shameless but I miss those days on the monte with you. I do not like to tell you the following but there has been almost no rain this year and our cow is thin for lack of grass. More happily—you will soon be an uncle as Mundo's wife Petra will give birth again in the next week or so—she is very thin too, never got fat like I did with Miguelito. Please write soon or call me at Don Rigoberto's house as he will send for me to come, and let me know about the stove.

I wish we were there with you and sometimes think of crossing the border with my Aunt Lidia next time she comes back just so we won't be apart anymore. My cousin Esther and her husband Jesús are thinking about crossing too. Your visit last spring made us happy but it was too short—Miguelito often asks where is my Papí, with his big brown eyes that look like yours, my sweet husband and I can only ask you to return soon or send for us. May you be well and may the Virgin always protect you.
Your loving wife,
Lucha

Six: **Antonio**

February, 1983

Antonio re-read Lucha's letter a several times, spelling out each
word with difficulty. He did not much like the idea of her going up
on the *monte*, even though her little brother was now old enough to
protect her. The *monte* was their special place, where they met and
loved before marrying and after. Lucha was such an attractive woman,
he reflected, with her wavy dark brown hair, her quick laugh, her ease
at talking to almost anyone. He had been jealous of her before, at
some dance or another when he had to relinquish her to a friend or
compadre, and she would look up at her partner with her almost sexy
laugh, her large full lips curving upward. What if one of the men from
the *rancho* tried to take advantage of his not being there and followed
her up to the *monte* and grabbed her and did the things he did with her
when they were there, beside that giant prickly pear cactus where he
had lain with her? He raged inside, a weight in his chest, a burning in
his stomach.

The next Sunday afternoon, when Nicolás and Ignacio had gone
out, down to Santa Monica pier, he arranged for Mundo and Edgar,
Lucha's brother, to stay at home with him. He wanted to bring up the
subject of his wife.

He sat at on the corner of the scuffy brown plastic sofa of the studio
apartment, where Edgar and Mundo took turns sleeping. The two sat
on faded grey fold up chairs in front of him. Antonio opened the first
six-pack of the two he had bought at the corner liquor store and offered
them to Mundo and Edgar. As usual Edgar refused the beer, opening up
a can of soda instead. They talked about work for awhile and getting
the money to pay next month's rent, then Antonio plunged in.

"Lucha wants to come over with me the next time I go back to the
rancho."

Mundo, his *tejana* in his lap, begins to worry the rim. "Do you think
she'll be able to make it?"

Antonio smiles and replies, "Lucha is like a mountain goat. I could
bring her across even in Tecate."

Mundo laughed. "You should know. All the times you took her
picking *nopales* up on the *monte*." He began tugging on his moustache.

Antonio, a look of surprise mixed with pride on his face, queries, "You knew we went up there together?"

Mundo answered, in a way he wouldn't have if they had not been on their second beer together, "Everyone knew, *hermano*. First Lucha would go up with the basket. And then a few minutes later you would disappear."

Hitting his hand on the arm of the already battered sofa , Antonio replied, "But she always took her little brother Rogelio!"

Mundo smiled. "Who knows what you did with him."

Edgar had been looking down at his folded hands, embarrassed about the turn in the conversation, not knowing whether to be angry with his sister for being the subject of such scandalous talk, not saying anything.

Mundo changed the subject then, seeing both Antonio's and Edgar's embarrassment. "I've heard from some guys from Jalisco that I met on Sawtelle that Tijuana is an easier crossing. Antonio leaned forward, his beer can in both hands, his elbows on his knees. "Tijuana. Lucha's cousin Esther's *tío* lives there. And Estela and Jesús have been wanting to cross over here too."

Mundo observes, "So you would have a place to stay. You might not even have to go back for her if she crosses with Esther and Jesús." He continued, "From what I heard you have to walk along the beach and some railroad tracks and climb a storm fence."

Antonio thought awhile. "I wouldn't want her to cross without me. It would be best to bring her across in March or April I guess. A couple of months to get the money together for the *coyote*. We would have to carry Miguelito, and she couldn't do that alone."

An image of the dead baby flashed through Mundo's head. "Why don't you leave Miguelito home with *mi Mamá*? Then go back and get him another time. After Lucha decides whether she wants to stay or not."

Antonio explains, hesitantly. "Lucha wants to be wherever I am. Since she was fourteen she always wanted to be with me. If she comes she will stay. And she'd never be separated from our son. Miguelito is her pride and joy." He was silent a moment. "And there are schools here. They go for six years and even more. Soon Miguelito will be school age."

Mundo did not challenge Antonio's decision. "We'll have to look for a larger place."

"Yep," Antonio replied. "There's a two room house for rent a couple of blocks down the street. If it's o.k. with you guys I am going to talk to the owner this evening."

Edgar smiled, walked to the door and looked out to the small green park a block over and across the way. When his sister came he would be able to send a message to Gabriela.

Seven: Lucha letter

West Los Angeles
May, 1983

My dearest Mamá, sister Berta and brother Rogelio,

I hope this letter finds you all in good health, as are my desires. I am writing from Los Angeles where we arrived more than a month ago. We were in Tijuana with my cousin Esther's uncle for almost two weeks before we crossed. It was a long walk, more than 15 kilometers and the first time we tried the migra caught us and sent us back to Tijuana. But first we were locked up beside Brownsfield Airfield for some hours and the migra didn't even offer us water. Then when they had caught enough people they loaded us all into a big bus and took us back across the border.

My beloved Antonio thought it was because we were carrying Miguelito and Esther and Jesús were carrying their little girl, Juanita, who is three and a bit gordita, and then Miguelito is four and heavy, so we couldn't run away fast enough. Esther's uncle had told us that we could sent the children with a coyote, that the coyote would cross them with birth certificates from children born in the United States, and bring them right to the house, but we didn't want to be separated from them. After we were caught though, and locked up, with the children crying and not even a piece of paper to wipe their poor little noses, we gave in. We dropped the children off with a couple. They told us they would take good care of the children, see that they got fed, told us to call once we were in Los Angeles. The next time we tried to cross everything went fine, a car picked us up in San Ysidro and we drove to Los Angeles and a nice house with an indoor sink and refrigerator and shower and toilet that Antonio had rented because we were coming. Esther and Jesús are staying with us until Jesús earns enough money for them to get a house of their own or an apartment. He has already found work as a carpenter's helper since he has worked at that before.

The worst thing about crossing was leaving the children and we got to Los Angeles and called the couple and they said it would be a few days. We didn't know we would be separated for so long, it was 5 days in all, but then on Wednesday the couple called and asked if we had the money for the children. And between my husband's uncle Ignacio, and his cousin

Nicolás, and his brother Mundo and my brother Edgar, we got together the 400 dollars, 200 dollars for each, Miguelito and Juanita. They were very sleepy when they got here and Juanita cried and Miguelito wanted to be held. But now we are together and Esther is looking after Miguelito so I can be looking for houses to clean.

We have a telephone in the house now that I am here, because Esther and I did not want to go to the apartment where the muchachos are living to make a call, as Antonio and Mundo did before I came, but I insisted we should have one for the house. So I can call patrones for example, or call you once in awhile. If you need to call me, or anyone needs to call us—we are Antonio and me, Esther and Jesús, Edgar and Nicolás and Ignacio living here right now, but Nicolás and Ignacio are thinking of going back to the apartment where they used to live—please give them this number 310 --- ----.

By the way I am now working cleaning two houses not far from where we live. I walked around the neighborhood asking everyone if they needed someone to clean their house, and two did. I wasn't here more than a week before finding work. I am also going to make tamales to sell in a nearby park.

May everything go well for all of you, and may the Virgin bless you, as are my desires.
Your daughter and sister,
Lucha

1985-1988

Lucha loved the little one bedroom house with its few meters of
lawn in front and the large backyard where she could hang clothes
to dry and even cook outside on the large, if rusty, grill the previous
tenants had left behind. All was new to her. She had never lived in
a house with running water, a sink and a shower and a bathtub, with
carpets on the floor, with glass windows, with electric lights in every
room, with a refrigerator. She still hadn't gotten used to it after almost
two years.

Antonio had left the apartment up the street to Ignacio and some
boys from the *rancho* who were living in Santa Monica and wanted
to move in to share the lower rent and be closer to Sawtelle. Mundo,
Nicolás and Edgar lived with Antonio and Lucha in the new house,
though sometimes Nicolás went to stay with his uncle Ignacio and
sometimes Ignacio, when he drank a lot, which was usual when he was
in Los Angeles, stayed overnight at Antonio's and Lucha's.

Edgar spent the first three weeks with his sister Lucha, before going
off to work in the office buildings on Pico at night, before saying
anything.

Then one day as she was seated in front of the television, a new and
wondrous thing Antonio had bought the week before, Edgar started
talking.

"How is your *cuñada* Gabriela?"

Lucha was put off a minute. What a strange question from Edgar,
who seldom asked about anybody. But she remembered that he had
often come to her in-laws' house, where she had lived with Antonio
after marrying, and where Gabriela lived. And there had been rumors
that he had eyes for Gabriela. But that was almost four years ago.

"Gabriela? She's doing fine. Still at home with my mother-in-law.
She helps her a lot." Then Lucha remembered another thing, "A
couple of times she asked me if I had heard from you."

Gathering his courage, Edgar said, "Lucha, I want you to help me
with a letter to her. I just don't know who to send it to."

"A letter" Lucha replied. "Well, we'll send it to my sister Berta.
Berta can read it to her and write back for her."

Lucha asked "Are you in love with her *hermano?*" She thought for a moment of Oníforo's constant visits to her in-laws' house. But that might be because his sister Petra, Mundo's wife, lived there too. Though he often asked Gabriela and only Gabriela to make him a cup of coffee. And once he had asked Gabriela, not Petra, to sew a shirt cuff that had come loose.

Edgar smiled, his elbows on his knees, turning his *tejana* in his hands, "Could be."

"*Ay hermano,* Lucha laughed happily, "let's get to it." She went out to the kitchen to get the notebook she had bought to write down the grocery lists and letters home. "Tell me what you want to say," she said, settling back in the dark grey sofa.

"Gabriela, my girl."

Lucha laughed, "You're not going to say 'my beloved'?"

Edgar blushed, looked down at the pale grey rug.

"Let's put Gabriela my beloved. What's next?"

He was silent for awhile, thinking. "I am coming back for our wedding soon. Probably in April or May the latest. It took me longer than I planned to earn the money."

"Edgar, you have plans to marry. How wonderful!"

Edgar put his head down again, twirled his *tejana* with two fingers. This was as hard as he had thought it would be.

"Anything else, Edgar?"

"No, that is all. Just my name," he replied.

Lucha signed it "Your sweetheart Edgar."

○

It would be another three months, in July, that someone they knew would return to the *rancho,* that someone could take a letter from Edgar to Gabriela, the envelope addressed to his sister Berta.

○

It was in August that they received a call from Oníforo, asking for Antonio. "*Hóla,* brother-in-law," he began.

"How are you?" Antonio answered, surprised that Oníforo would call him brother-in-law. It was Mundo who was married to Oníforo's sister, not him.

"Hear this," said Oníforo, "I have news. And I didn't invite you because we didn't have a real wedding. Just the civil registry. Hear this, I married your sister Gabriela. Three months ago."

Antonio felt his stomach lurch. Why hadn't someone told them? His mother could have had someone write. Or could have called from Don Rigoberto's. Unless she was not happy about it.

"Hear this. Gabriela is expecting and I lost my job with the cows."

Antonio remembered that Oyelo, hear this, as they called Oníforo, always missed days of work no matter what job he did. "Isn't the harvest coming up soon?" he asked.

"It's not doing so good this year. *Mi jefe* can take care of it alone."

Antonio waited. Oníforo always talked on an on.

"Look here, brother-in-law, I would like to come across, try to find a good paying job there, if you will pay the *coyote*. Maybe next month."

Antonio thought a moment, about adding Oníforo to the household. But he had to think of his sister's welfare. "Sure *cuñado*," he finally said, almost choking over the word. "Be glad to help you out."

"What's up," Mundo asked, when Antonio got off the phone.

Antonio shook his head, put his face in his hands, and then said, "Oyelo's coming."

"*Ay cabrón*," said Mundo, and then "it will be lucky if we get the *coyote*'s fees back from him."

"Worse," Antonio replied. "He's married Gabriela."

○

Antonio now knew from Lucha that Edgar was in love with their youngest sister, Gabriela. And Edgar was a more reliable, more responsible, all around nicer *muchacho*. Antonio felt a loss. So did Mundo, even though he was married to Oniforo's sister.

Lucha did not know what to tell her brother. He was so shy and honest and kind-hearted, just like Gabriela. Lucha had learned over the past weeks that one of Edgar's reasons for crossing to Los Angeles was to earn money for his and Gabriela's wedding, not just to send money back to their widowed mother. But he had stayed longer than the two years he thought he would be gone, more than four years now.

O

Berta's answering letter arrived a few weeks later with the return of one of the *muchachos* who shared the apartment with Ignacio. Berta wrote that Gabriela did not have anything to say to Edgar, but that when she read Gabriela Edgar's letter, Gabriela burst into tears and said, "I'm sorry. I'm so sorry." Berta also wrote that Oníforo did not treat Gabriela very well and she was often red-eyed in the morning. That Oníforo often went to dances on nearby *ranchos* and did not take Gabriela along. That once he came home drunk and threw all the clothes Gabriela had washed and ironed on the dirt floor in the kitchen, telling her to wash them again. That Gabriela's eyes were getting worse, and she could hardly see to thread a needle. That, on a happier note, they had received Lucha's letter as well and could not believe the things she had seen. And Berta asked if Lucha now washed her hair with shampoo.

O

Edgar stayed in his sister Lucha and brother-in-law Antonio's house, where he had lived since arriving in Los Angeles, for only a day after Oníforo came to join the family. Edgar could not stand Oníforo's vulgarity and posturing, his constant desire to be the center of attention. And he was Gabriela's husband now. Edgar's pleasingly plump, quiet, shy Gabriela. The reason he had come to the United States, to earn money for their wedding and to build a house for her.

Edgar knew Oníforo took precedence in Antonio's household, even though Oníforo was not well liked. He was Antonio's sister's husband, and Antonio was the household head and breadwinner, even though Lucha helped out by cleaning houses. He was also Mundo's wife's brother. He himself was only Antonio's wife's brother. No one needed to ask him to leave. He packed up the small brown cardboard suitcase he had bought at the second-hand store on Sawtelle, filled it with his work clothes, bought at the same store, and asked Antonio to give him a ride up the street to Apartment 25, where a whole slew of men from the *rancho* lived, including Antonio's cousin Nicolás and tío Ignacio, both of whom Edgar got along well with.

He and Antonio exchanged only a few words along the way. "So you are leaving us," Antonio said.

"Yes," said Edgar, "It's time for me to move in with the boys."

Antonio, after a long pause, replied, "*Lo siento*. I'm sorry. I'm sorry things worked out the way they did." For a second, Edgar's eyes stung.

Gabriela and their son, Moíses, followed Oníforo to Lucha and Antonio's house three months later. Antonio and Mundo pooled their money to pay for the *coyote*, as Oníforo had not found steady work for his first two months in the city, and worked only three day a week, maybe four. But good luck had come his way. A recruiter had arrived on day when Oníforo was standing on Sawtelle and waiting for some *patrón* to come by. The recruiter picked up twenty of the younger men to work in an airplane parts factory. Oníforo was one of them. He had worked there for a month and planned to do so for at least two more months so he and Gabriela and Moíses could look for a place of their own. Meanwhile they would stay with Antonio and Lucha and Miguelito and Mundo, in their one-bedroom house, sleeping on the floor in the living room.

Miguelito's birthday was coming up in June and as usual Antonio and Lucha put on a party for him. Oníforo and Gabriela and Moíses were still living in Antonio's house, but Edgar came to the party with Nicolás and Ignacio. He sat silently in a corner, twisting his beer bottle in his hands, picking the label off of it, looking toward Gabriela, with whom he had had no conversation except an exchange of greetings, whenever he thought she was not looking at him. Gabriela had heard from Lucha that Edgar had planned to earn money to make her his bride. She had never imagined it. He had never declared himself. Occasionally she stole a glance at him. He would indeed, with his polite ways, have been a better husband than Oníforo, who seemed to enjoy insulting and humiliating her not just when they were alone but in front of people.

She remembered how, only a few months after they were married, he began to go out to dances on nearby *ranchos*, leaving her at home with her mother, in whose house they lived. On nights when he would go to the dances he would come into the house and order her to iron such and such a shirt and such and such a pants. One day she had washed almost all of his clothing, six pants and six shirts, and he ordered her to iron the dark green pearl buttoned one, and she obediently went to do so. When she handed him the shirt, he grabbed it, said she had done a lousy job, that she didn't know how to be a wife, and threw it down on the dirt floor of the house. Then he went over to the laundry basket in which his newly washed clothes were carefully folded and dumped everything on the floor, stamped on them, ground them into the floor. "Now get out and wash them again," he had told her. And she went outside, as evening was approaching, and filled the washing tub, her tears falling into the water as she washed his clothes for the second time that day.

As she got bigger with their baby, he used to taunt her. "You'd like to go to the dance too, right?" After she would nod, he would say, "Who wants to go with a pregnant woman. You wouldn't even keep your feet under you, less be able to dance."

At the party Edgar noticed Oníforo's dismissive and demeaning attitude toward Gabriela. Oníforo would call out, "Hear me, *vieja.* Bring me another beer." And she would stop whatever she was doing or get up from wherever she was sitting and go out to the refrigerator and bring him a beer. That wasn't unusual as Lucha did the same for Antonio, most any woman did the same for her man, but it was the manner in which he asked, as though he were her master and she his servant. And then when she brought it to him, he just grabbed it out of her hand without even looking at her or saying "*Gracías.*"

Sometimes, when she would try to add to a conversation Oníforo would tell her to just shut up or say that it was a stupid remark, sometimes turning to her and asking "Do you know how stupid you sound?" And Gabriela would just hug Moíses closer to her, if he were sitting on her lap, or just look down, stare at the carpet.

Mundo and Antonio were often out of earshot, or engaged in conversations when he insulted Gabriela, but they would not have interfered any way, as Gabriela had married Oníforo of her own free will. She had made her bed and must lie in it. She was unlucky in her marriage, but so were many other women. That was their destiny.

Edgar felt terrible, partially because he had lost her and partially because of the *mala vida* she was living. He would have treated her better, she was his love, he would have given her the respect a woman hopes for from a man. He would have given her a better life than Oníforo.

Oníforo and Gabriela and Moíses eventually moved to a rented row house in Venice, just one room and an attached kitchen. But there were more parties, usually at Antonio's house, to which they came and to which Edgar came. Edgar, who tended not to talk much in any case,

remained almost silent at the parties. He had heard that Oníforo was
going out to the bars and leaving Gabriela at home with their son. He
felt badly for her, though other men also did this sometimes as well.
He wouldn't have. He would have taken her dancing. Every week if
possible. He had danced with her at some of the dances on the *rancho*,
had danced with her the month before he came to Los Angeles. He
had loved dancing with her, holding her in his arms as she smiled
shyly up at him. But aside from that, Oníforo was irresponsible with
everyone. He never paid the money for the *coyote* back to Antonio and
Mundo.

Edgar decided that he could not continue witnessing such abuse
toward the Gabriela he still loved. And there was no way he could
run away with her. Both of them would lose their families. Whatever
relative he joined, rumors would eventually get back to Oníforo. And
thus Oníforo would hunt them down, especially if they took Moisés. As
a matter of pride rather than of sentiment, Edgar suspected. More abuse
would follow for Gabriela. Oníforo would beat her for her infidelity and
her running away would just give him license to heap more abuse on
her. And even her mother and sister would think he had the right to
do so.

So one day Edgar called his Aunt Lidia in Chicago, the aunt who
had left her husband and worked cleaning and old peoples' home, and
asked her if there was work for him in that city. "Come on out and
we'll find you something," she answered, glad that she might have
the company of her favorite nephew. So Edgar left, shortly before
Christmas, for the Pilsen district in Chicago.

Nine: **Luís**

1986

Luís was the eldest of his sibling group. Nicolás followed him by two years and his little sister Juana by 10 years. In between there had been another brother and sister. He always remembered his mother's grief as she held first one and then the other of their dying bodies close to her chest. Neither had reached the age of two before the diarrhea that dried them out, whitened their skin, and led to their bones protruding, eventually killed them.

When Luís had reached his 19th birthday, he still had no *novia*. He had twice gone with some of the boys to visit prostitutes in Fresnillo, but he felt that there was a coldness he didn't like in the transaction. As the eldest, Luís had no elder brother to teach him how to woo or even to suggest whom to woo. Luís was older than his cousin Antonio, who at age 15 was the eldest of *his* sibling group, so he didn't even have a cousin to turn to. All he knew was that men and women grew to a certain age, got a sweetheart, married that sweetheart, and had as many children as God sent.

There was a pretty girl who for the past few months had come once or twice a week to the *tiendita*, where after their day's work in the fields the *muchachos* assembled to drink a soda or a beer. Or perhaps nothing, unless they could get credit, if they had no pesos to spend. She would nod to them and say *"Buenas tardes,"* as she held the hand of the child who accompanied her, and they would answer, almost in unison, *"Buenas tardes."* Luís began tipping his *tejana* to her when she walked by. No one was sure who she was, but they knew she sometimes came to visit Antonio's aunt Renata and that she lived on a nearby *rancho*.

Renata was a widow. She had been the second wife of Antonio's father's brother, Don Nato. His first wife had died giving birth to their third child and soon afterwards Don Nato had married a young woman only 18 years old at the time, from the *rancho* Santa María, 15 kilometers away. They did not have children together for some years, and there were whispers that she was barren, but what did it matter, because she now mothered Nato's two daughters and treated them well. Then, in a period of four years she gave birth to three daughters. The eldest was only seven when Don Nato, shortly after his 50th birthday, died of a heart attack right after having crossed over the Tecate mountains and arriving at his destination in Los Angeles.

Renata was an outsider, but as the youngest of her family, she had no place to go. Her two older brothers had large families of their own and could not take her in. Her parents had died by the time she was 30. Here in Santa Martha she had a house and a hectare of land she let out for sharecropping. She was also an outsider because at times one or two men would arrive from other *ranchos* and get drunk and who knew what else in her small two room house. That's how she made money to support the five children some said, some in disgust, some in sympathy, a few in admiration. It turned out that the pretty young girl who came to the *tiendita* was her eldest brother's eldest daughter, who came to help her with the clothes washing and the maize grinding, and other chores.

Luís decided he could do well enough marrying her. She was polite. She was pretty. She had no sweetheart. She was his age. He finally asked his cousin Antonio to ask his sister Lucy—when Lucy came back to the *rancho* on week-ends from her house cleaning job in Fresnillo— to find her name out for him. And Antonio asked Lucy. And Lucy, who kept up with all the gossip on the *rancho*, already knew her name. It was Laura. And she had no *novio*. She had no elder brothers or sisters. A younger brother had joined his uncle in Guadalajara to work in a shoe-making shop.

Luís knew that within some months there would be a dance on the *rancho*. Someone would get married, or there would be a baptism, or someone would like to celebrate something. And this would occur at the end of the harvest, in October, both in Santa Martha and in the neighboring *ranchos*. Laura, without a brother to watch over her, would probably not go to the dances on *ranchos* other than her own, unless her parents took her. But, with her connection to Renata, she would surely be present at any dance in Santa Martha.

A dance was finally held in October, when Don Anulfo came back from Los Angeles to harvest his fields and to celebrate the marriage of his youngest son to a girl from the nearby *rancho* Santa Marta. And Luís danced with Laura a number of times. The first dance or two they danced in silence. Then, he asked her, "Do you have a *novio?*" though he knew she did not.

"No," she answered looking up at him with her heavy-lashed dark eyes, and with a little smile.

He waited awhile before he asked "Would you like to have a *novio*?"

"Depends who," she replied teasingly.

"Me," Luís answered blushing.

She gave him a big smile and softly answered, "*Sí.*"

And thus did their *noviazgo* begin. Since his father had died, Luís asked his tío Ignacio to come with him to represent his case to Laura's parents. They carried the traditional bottle of liquor and knocked on the door. Laura's father answered and invited them to sit on the small front porch with him. They talked about the harvest. The bottle remained unopened. Laura's father asked Luís who his father was. "Don Estebán, but he is deceased."

Laura's father looked a bit surprised. "Don Estebán from Santa Martha? We crossed the border together. As *braceros*. In 1955, before I was married. Then again in 1956. We worked the cotton in Texas together. He was a good man."

Laura's father called to his wife, "Bring us some glasses Anita."

The three sat and drank a toast to Don Estebán. Then Ignacio broached the subject of why they were here. "Don Estebán's son, this youngster here, Luís, would like to ask for your daughter Laura in marriage."

Laura's father looked serious for a while, looked out over the fields in the distance. Then he took a sip from his glass, reached his hand out to Luís and said, "As long as you treat her well, you are welcome to our family, son."

At the end of the following year's harvest they married, and every near harvest season after that for three years, they had a child. It was right after his third child was born that Luís, whose two hectares of land did not produce enough corn to support his growing family, decided to look for work in Los Angeles. He asked Don Anulfo if he could accompany him, and Don Anulfo said yes.

Luís found work as a gardener and did not return to the *rancho* for two years. He brought his wife and children many presents—mostly clothing from the second-hand store, but also a battery-powered radio-cassette player and a hand-held mirror. He stayed on the *rancho* for two months, sowing his *ejido* land and leaving his brother Nicolás in charge of harvesting it. When he left again, he left Laura pregnant with their fourth child. His cousin Antonio accompanied him north, and soon got a job as a gardener too. Two years later Luís again returned, for he would have lost his *ejido* rights if the land remained unplanted for more than two years. When he left once more for Los Angeles, his cousin Mundo and his brother Nicolás and his *tío* Ignacio came along.

It was some time before his last crossing that he had met Sara.

Luís, during his years on the *rancho* married to Laura had gotten used to waking up to the warmth of a woman at his side. He didn't like to visit prostitutes both because it took money away from the funds he could sent to his family, but also because he was affectionate and craved affection, a thing missing if sometimes pretended in the monetary transaction. But also because their stories were often so sad that it bothered him that he could not do more than buy them a couple of drinks and give them $25 after the coupling.

Sometimes the boys would go down to the bar on Olympic Boulevard where a Mexican band played on Saturday nights. They could dance with the bar girls. After the dancing, or in between dances, the girls would ask for a drink. Their drinks looked like miniature beers, but cost twice as much as a regular beer. The girls earned a dollar each drink, and would spend about half an hour at the table while they drank each one, unless a girl really liked one of the boys, and hoped to get him to invite her to the hotel across the street. That cost a good bit however, $25 for the room, usually rented by the hour, and $25 for the girl. Sometimes girls would come to Apartment 25, and the other Mexican-inhabited apartments in the two-story complex, so that it wasn't necessary to go to the bar at all. But listening to the band and dancing was a worthwhile pastime, most thought.

When Luís first went to the bar, with two of the boys from Apartment 25, he saw a girl who reminded him of his sister Juana. He asked her to dance and found out she too was from Zacatecas. He politely asked her if she would like a drink, and she came to sit with the three men for a while. Luís, after some minutes, asked her how she came to work in this bar.

"My husband crossed the border five years ago, leaving me with two little ones. We never heard from him again. I did not know if he died on crossing. Or if he couldn't get anyone to write a letter for him. Two years after he left I came to Tijuana with my little sister. There was no work for us there. I had only finished two years of schooling and the *maquiladoras* wanted girls who had finished at least primary school. I told my sister I would find a way to support us, and I began working in a bar for a dollar a drink. I did that for almost two years."

She did not tell them that the buyers of drinks often were few, and occasionally she let a man take her to a hotel down to street to make ends meet.

"And how did you get to Los Angeles?" Luís asked.

"A man who used to come into the bar about once or twice a month asked me if I wanted to cross and do the same work here. I thought that would bring me closer to my husband, not that he would want anything to do with me now, so I accepted."

"Did you come alone?" Luís asked.

"With my two little ones and my sister, who cares for them. We crossed right over the line with false papers. And then the *coyote* drove us here and the man, who is the owner of this bar, let us stay in his house until I earned enough money to rent a room. He was nice. He didn't expect anything of me except to work here and give him a percentage of what I earn. But if I leave before five years I will have to pay him back for the *coyote*."

"Where do you live here?" Luís asked, unaware that he should not have been so forward, or perhaps made forward by the two beers he had consumed.

"In Cozy Corners," she replied."

The boys knew the infamous *vecindad* on Sawtelle, even had friends from the *rancho* living there. Tiny rooms surrounded a courtyard, each room with a hotplate, a bathroom made for slender midgets, with only a toilet. One washed one's hands or bathed in the kitchen sink.

When they left, Luís handed her a $20 bill, but had no thoughts of taking her across the street to the motel. She reminded him too much of Juana.

If he could have he would have brought his pretty Laura and the five children to Los Angeles. But there was no way he could afford to keep them there, and the children were too young for Laura to go out to work to help him with the rent. As it was he paid one-tenth of the $550 monthly rent for Apartment 25, shared with 9 other *muchachos* from the *rancho*. He could do half of that, but not more. The whole rent would be more than two weeks of pay and they would have to eat and buy clothing and pay doctors and, in sum, they would barely be better off than on the *rancho*. And also, the city was no place to raise his *chamacos*. There were drug dealers all around, and gangs.

He loved the *rancho*, and would have returned if there had been a way to support the family there. But there was not. He came to realize that for most of his working life, Laura and the children would be on the *rancho*, and he would be in Los Angeles.

Aside from her glossy auburn hair, which reminded Luís of a mare his father once had, Sara was not as pretty as Laura. But she combined an understated sensuality with a fragility, and yet a strength.

Sara was two years older than he was. She had come from El Salvador three years ago and lived with a half-brother near MacArthur Park. Sometimes on Friday and Saturday evenings she worked in a small El Salvadorean restaurant near Wilshire Boulevard, and four days a week she cleaned houses in Beverly Hills. Her husband had been killed during the civil war, and she left for Los Angeles less than a year later. She had a 15-year-old son living with her mother in San Salvador.

Whenever the boys from Apartment 25 could find a ride, and after Antonio bought his pick-up that was sometimes from him, they went to the Sunday rodeo in El Monte. It was a Mexican rodeo and it was followed by a dance with a Mexican band. One week-end the owners of the El Salvadorean restaurant brought Sara and her brother. She danced with Luís for the first time there.

They met there again, as they had agreed upon, two weeks later. Luís asked her if she would like to see a movie with him the following week, and she said yes. After the movie—a Mexican one about undocumented workers crossing the border—they went to a 24-hour restaurant and talked, talked for hours. Sara had lived in the countryside as a child and a young woman, so they had things in common to talk about: the joy of riding horseback in the fields, the beauty of the sunset, the vulnerability of the maize. It was not until they had stayed a night together that Sara told him about things he had never seen: soldiers cutting down men, women, and children after hauling them off buses, soldiers setting fire to the small house in the village where she had lived before the family fled to San Salvador. Her husband's body dumped in front of the house they rented in the capital, his back and neck torn apart with a machete. Her desire to bring her son to Los Angeles.

At times, when they spent the night together, she woke up sobbing. When Luís embraced her and asked what was wrong, she told him of her recurring nightmare. The village on fire and her son inside of the burning shack. She needs to run to get to him before he is consumed by the flames. But as great her effort might be, she could not get any nearer to the house.

For some months they saw each other on week-ends, and then Sara asked Luís if he would like to move in. For Sara and her brother it meant paying less rent, for Luís more. But Luís found in Sara the warmth he needed, a wife away from the *rancho*. So he moved into their small apartment in the Pico-Union area. He continued to work as a gardener, and that meant he had to get up an hour earlier, to take the bus down Wilshire to Federal Avenue, where his boss picked him up near the Federal building. Then a long bus ride back to Pico-Union after work. They needed a maid in one of the houses where he did gardening work, and he recommended Sara. Sara then had five days a week of work, and stopped waitressing in the restaurant. She did not expect money from him. His earnings went to his family in Mexico. Her earnings went to an account to bring her son to Los Angeles from San Salvador.

Rumors about activities in Los Angeles went back to the *rancho* via phone calls, letters, and people returning for visits, short or extended. Lucy made sure that Laura would know about Luís and Sara.

Laura cried after hearing about it, but didn't know if it was true or merely idle gossip, would not know until she talked to Luís. She called him several times at Apartment 25, but the boys just told her he was out. The place she phoned from closed at 8 p.m., so she never knew how late he was out, or the fact that he was living elsewhere.

Mundo had come back to the *rancho* for a couple of months, and was getting ready to head north again with some of the boys. Laura decided to write to Luís and ask him what was going on.

My dearest husband,
I hope this letter finds you in good health, as are my desires. Your wife
and children are well. I do not know how to begin, but I will just do so.
I do not know if it is just gossip or if it is true, but some on the rancho
are saying you have abandoned us and now have another woman. I do
not believe it is true because you sent us money with Mundo when he
returned. I love you my husband, and hope it is not true. Remember we
gave vows to be together forever.
Please write and let me know it is not true.
I remain faithfully yours,

Your wife,
Laura."
p.s. Our cow now has a new calf.

When Luís received the letter, he decided it would be best to go back and talk to his wife face-to-face and a week later he left, after putting one of the boys who got work on Sawtelle in his place at the houses where he was employed as a gardener, and after telling Sara he would be back in a month. "I must go and talk to her, and let her know I will never completely abandon them," Luís told Sara.

Sara took his hands into, drew him to her and kissed him lightly. "Of course you must go," she said, "but please come back safely."

Luís, accompanied by his brother Nicolás, who as usual could not miss the chance to see his wife, took a bus from downtown Los Angeles to El Paso and then walked across the border. From El Paso they took a bus to Fresnillo, and from there another bus to Santa Martha. It took them more than two days.

Laura was happy to see him, though he was too tired to talk much, and went to their bed to sleep for the next 12 hours. When he awoke at about 9 a.m., Laura had made him one of his favorite breakfasts: hot chocolate and tacos of *nopal* and onions in a red chile sauce.

Luís ate quietly. Afterwards he said, "We must talk."

Laura looked a bit fearful but came to sit beside him on the bed, their only real piece of furniture, their table made of orange crates and boards.

Luís took her hand, and said, "I will never leave you Laura. I will never abandon our children."

Laura smiled tentatively, "Then it is not true you have a woman in Los Angeles?"

"You don't want to come north with me, Laura. Life in the city is rough and I cannot afford to keep our family there."

"Then come back to the *rancho*. Sow your lands, and we will make it somehow."

"You know that no one with just two hectares of *milpa* can support a family here in Santa Martha."

Tears welled up in Laura's eyes. "What then?"

Luís pulled her to him. "I miss your warmth. I miss the warmth of a woman."

"So it is true?"

"I am living with a widow from El Salvador. We help each other out."

Laura pulled away, looked at him, tears falling.

"Then you don't want us, your family, anymore," she choked.

"I will always love you and my children. I will always send money so you will not go hungry or want for clothes or fees for my children's schooling. I will always come back to visit, as I have always done. You are my wife and one day, if possible, we will live together again here on the *rancho*." Only the last sentence was doubtful, for Luís thought, there was no way for them to live together on the *rancho* and not starve. Every household on the *rancho* had at least one person in the United States, other than the whole households that had moved elsewhere in Mexico, to Guadalajara or a border city. Maybe one or more of his sons would replace him when they were grown. But each only for a few years, since they too would marry and need to support their own households.

When Laura realized what it all meant, that he loved them but could not be with them, that he missed her and thus took another woman to his bed, she sobbed and sobbed. She would not speak to him the rest of the day, just shook her head when he spoke to her, tears welling.

He took her to a movie in Fresnillo, walked hand-in-hand with her as couples in the United States did. They went up on the *monte* to gather tuna and *nopales*, together with their children. Laura made tacos so they could a picnic on the highest hill. They went over to the old hacienda and picked the giant apples from a vast unattended orchard. They did not talk about Los Angeles again, until the day before Luís was to go back. Luís took Laura in his arms, that night, and said to Laura, "There is something I want to tell you. They are talking about giving papers to us *mojados* who have lived in the United States since 1980. I have been there since 1977. They call it *amnesía*. If I get my amnesty I will come back every year to see you, maybe twice a year, to be with you and the children. I won't have to pay a *coyote* and you won't have to worry about what could happen to me when I cross the border."

Laura gave him a smile almost like the one she had given him when he asked if he could be her *novio*. She held him tightly and replied, "You are my husband and I will always love you."

"But you must promise to call me every week," she added.

Luís took her into his strong arms and said, "You are my wife and I will always love you, too. And I will call you every week." They understood that theirs was a fate they would not have chosen, had economic conditions been otherwise.

Ten: **Lucy**

1987

Lucy came north with her brother Mundo, when he returned from his visit to the *rancho* in January of 1987, and moved in with Antonio and Lucha and Mundo and Lucha helped find her work cleaning houses. She came to clean one house in Beverly Hills twice a week, and two different houses in West Los Angeles on two different days.

Lucy had seen a certain young man every Tuesday and Thursday on her way back from Beverly Hills where she worked as a domestic and he was a gardener like her brothers. She got on the bus first, then he got on one stop down. He was slightly overweight like her brother Antonio but unlike her brothers he did not have a moustache. He did have penetrating almost yellow eyes framed in long dark brown eyelashes. And a quick sunburst of a smile.

In the beginning they just eyed one another. Then one Thursday, as he got on the bus, Lucy smiled at him. And he flashed a smile back. Next Tuesday when he got on the bus the seat beside her was empty and he chose it.

"You're a pretty woman," he said, his eyes lingering on her high cheekbones and aquiline nose.

Lucy looked down at her hands, twisted the gold ring she was buying on an installment plan from one of Lucha's aunts. It was adorned with a small amethyst, her birth stone. *"Favor que me hace,"* she replied in a soft low voice.

"Where are you from?," he asked her.

"Zacatecas," she said, her eyes cast down. She did not want him to think she was easy.

"Zacatecas, Zacatecas?" he asked, a way of throwing her the flower of sophistication, pretending not to guess that she was from some poverty-stricken *rancho*, as most Mexicans he knew in Los Angeles were.

"No. From a small *rancho* near Fresnillo. Do you know Zacatecas?"

"Only from passing through. One time when I went to visit my sister in Ciudad Juárez. Looking for a job in the *maquiladoras*. They weren't hiring men then." He paused, as though awaiting a comment, but when none came he added, "I'm from Guerrero."

Lucy looked at him sideways. "You don't look *indio*."

He chuckled. "Not all of us from Guerrero are *indios*."

She said, flushing, "Sometimes they call us *indios*. Because we live on a *rancho*." She paused, fingered her ring again. "But we speak only Spanish. And our saint is the *Niño de Atocha*."

"I'm José Hernández, *para servirle*." José extended his hand, reaching across his chest and hers.

"Lucy Contreras, *para servirle*," she answered, taking his hand. He pressed her small wash wrinkled hand briefly before releasing it.

When it came time for him to get off, three stops before hers on Santa Monica Boulevard, he touched his baseball cap with two fingers and said, "*Hasta luego*. Until then."

From then on, on Tuesdays and Thursdays Lucy always chose a seat where there was an empty one beside her, and José always sat with her. They talked about television programs they liked, the places they knew in the city of Los Angeles, and the problems they faced when they crossed the border and first arrived in the United States.

Over a soda in an outdoor restaurant on Sawtelle Boulevard, near where José lived, they talked about their families. José shared an apartment with two brothers and three cousins. They had all crossed within the last three years. He had relatives elsewhere in California, some cousins in Santa Barbara and an uncle in Lompoc. "One of my cousins always likes to drink too much on Saturday night. Then he wants to go to a dance. But they don't have dances here like they do in Guerrero."

Nor like they do in Zacatecas, Lucy told him. People arriving on horseback from nearby *ranchos*. Or on burros. Even women. Sometimes with their husbands, sometimes looking for a *novio*. At times someone shot off a pistol, which led others to shoot off theirs. Even her youngest brother had done that once.

Once Lucy told him about Manuel, her father's brother's son from a nearby *rancho* who lived in Apartment 25. "One of my cousins never went to school. His father needed him to work on the *parcela*. And then we only had two years of elementary school on our *rancho*. So he didn't learn how to read. He called us up the first week he was here and told us the *mayordomo* hadn't come for him to take him home that day. And he didn't know the bus routes. 'Can you come and pick me up?,' he said. My brother Antonio has a pick-up. 'Where are you?,'" my brother Antonio asked him. 'In front of the supermarket,' he replied. 'What supermarket? What street?' Well Manuel didn't know how to read the name of the street or the name of the supermarket. So he had to wait, holding onto the phone, until he found a Mexican passing by who could read and tell us where he was."

José shook his head, smiled. "The problems we face here," he said, and pressed Lucy's knee with his own. Then, "What kind of pick-up does your brother have?"

"An old Ford. Light blue. Have you seen it? He and my brother Mundo work gardening in Pacific Palisades and on Saturday in Beverly Hills."

José realized then that Lucy's brothers were the ones who had stolen the Saturday Beverly Hills garden from he and his brother. They hadn't had a pick-up and that could haul the gardening tools. They didn't even have many gardening tools. And the owner wanted them to bring their own. They probably could have negotiated something, since they had worked there three weekends already using the owners lawn mowers and other tools. But then the men in the light blue Ford pick-up arrived and offered to do the gardening. So they lost the business.

"Could be," José replied to Lucy.

They continued seeing each other for the next few weeks, drinking sodas every Thursday after work at Margarita's cafe on Sawtelle. Once Lucy sneaked away one Saturday, saying that one of her employers wanted her to work an extra day, and she and José spent the day on Santa Monica pier, then walked hand in hand down to Venice Beach to catch the bus home from there. Occasionally José put an arm around her shoulders. That day was the first she had kissed him.

One Thursday José asked Lucy if she would like to go with him to Lompoc to meet an uncle of his who worked there in the flower fields. Lucy knew her brothers would never give her permission to go away for a week-end, even with a female friend. She had been afraid to tell them about José. They didn't like Guerrerenses for one thing. Too much job competition. And the customs were different. They didn't like people from Sinaloa either. Mundo had even asked if they were really Mexicans, or came from some other country. Their women swore and smoked and drank like men and wore revealing blouses and even miniskirts. Things a respectable woman from Zacatecas would never be allowed to do. Lucy had seen a nice sleeveless dress in the second hand store on Sawtelle, where she and Lucha did almost all their clothes shopping, but she had known not to buy it. Dresses had to be at least knee length and with sleeves.

And then her brothers would never let her leave the house for a week-end because they, like all the men from their *rancho*, were always afraid their womenfolk would do something to bring them shame. Back on the *rancho* a woman, married or not, could not even go to the store to buy tortillas alone. She had to borrow a child to accompany her, or wait for a sister or brother.

And yet they had brought her here to the United States. Did they doubt that she wanted to marry? Didn't they suspect she would meet someone here?

José and Lucy planned to leave Friday night after they both finished working. Lucy always brought a change of clothes to work with her, so no one thought it strange when she left the house with a plastic bag containing an extra dress and high heels.

○

In Lompoc José took Lucy to the park to admire the low riders, with their pin-striping and multicolored paintings. Her favorites were the red Chevrolet painted with the Mexican serpent and eagle and the green Buick with the Virgin of Guadalupe. Then he took her to various bars with Mexican music on the juke box to dance to. They danced body pressed against body and sat embraced between dances, and José's uncle seemed to like her. In one of the bars, when they were listening to one of the Bukis love songs, a photographer came around and José had a picture taken of them, embracing, empty and half full beer bottles in the foreground. He gave the photograph to Lucy. "So you'll remember me," he said.

Saturday night they slept together on a small cot José's uncle put up for them in the kitchen. Lucy hoped José was drunk enough not to notice she was not a virgin. She had told him about a *novio* she had had for a long time. That they had planned to marry, but then his family moved to Mexico City. It was as good a story as any, and he could decide how far they had gone. In actuality she had not been a virgin for a longer time than anyone knew. Not since her uncle Efraím had grabbed her inside the cow shed the day after she turned nine years old. She had never told anyone about that, though for some months she burst into tears every time she saw him walking through the *rancho*.

Uncle Efraím had been shot down at a dance on a distant *rancho* a few years later. He died in a pool of his own blood, they said.

In any case, she pretended it hurt when José entered her, muffled small screams like those Uncle Efraím had muffled with his handkerchief, this time a pretended echo.

José said nothing about the night before the next morning.

Her sleep had been troubled. She could not sleep for an hour or more after they made love, though José seemed to have fallen asleep immediately. And when she slept she had one of her recurrent dreams. Lucy dreamed she walked hand in hand with a man in a field filled with wild grasses and daisies and *manzanilla* flowers. She could not see the man's face at first—it was a blur, but she knew that he was her *novio* and would one day be her husband. He asked her to wait for him in one corner of the field, not far from a cluster of trees and bushes, and told her he would be right back. She waited and waited, but he did not come back. Then, from behind the bushes, she saw her uncle walking toward her, the alcoholic uncle who had raped her. And feeling very alone, she turned to run, back to somewhere—somewhere where there were people who could protect her from him. She couldn't think of the name of her *novio* to call to him for help. She remembered who he was now, though. He was the nephew of a woman she had worked for in Fresnillo. The one who had paid her such attention, only later to marry another, bringing the girl to the house when Lucy was there, to present to his aunt. So she had to leave that job, a good job, with a kindly employer, to save her pride. And in the dream her uncle kept getting closer, even though her legs were like a deer's as she bounded and hopped and jumped to get away from him, hopped and skipped through the daisy and *manzanilla* filled fields. But no matter how fast she bounded and ran, her uncle was getting closer. Then she tripped. And her uncle was upon her, pulling at her clothes, like it was back in the stable when she was seen, and she couldn't get away from him no matter how much she fought and fought. And there was no one around to help her. She awoke, and found herself twisted in the sheet that had covered her and José. She heard him laughing with his uncle in the kitchen.

On the bus trip back to Los Angles, Lucy, planning for the wedding sure to come, told José, "You must come to meet my brothers. My cousins. My uncle Ignacio." She elbowed him in a gesture of flirtation, "I want to introduce them to my official *novio*."

José gazed out the window. Then he said, almost cruelly, "I already have a wife. And three children. In Guerrero." He had no plans to continue the relationship in any case. There were other pretty women. The excitement was in the chase. She hadn't been a virgin in any case. But she had served to wreak vengeance on her brothers' robbery of his and his brother's gardening job.

O

Lucy wandered the streets for hours after getting off at the bus station in Santa Monica. Once again she had been made a fool of. Once again she had no one. She sat for awhile on a bench in Santa Monica park, until night fell. And she remembered her other recurrent dream. She would dream she was on the *rancho*, walking toward the queen's stage in a long white dress with a frilly skirt, belt and neck trimmed with the brightest red roses. She would dream she had been elected queen of the *ranchos* in the competition among *señoritas* that occurred most years, right after the harvest. She walked, with a bouquet of red roses, hands in front of her belt, just a bit lower, like Veronica Castro, calling attention to that secret place all men seemed to want, toward the stage, where she would be crowned by those from her *rancho* and nearby *ranchos* who had also elected their candidates for queen-ship. She smiled, turning her face from side to side, brought the roses up to sniff them, held them at her breast for a few seconds, then returned them to below her belt. She dreamed she would be queen. All the young men would want to court her. As she reached the first step of the stairway up to the makeshift wooden stage, decorated here and there with daisies and roses, someone called out "She's no *señorita*." "Only a *señorita* can be queen." Lucy felt her hands tremble, her face flush. Lucha and Petra, still not married, were there, also queen candidates. The crown would go to one of them, or to her sister Gabriela. "She's no *señorita*" an anonymous man yelled once more. Lucy threw the roses to one side, turned to run, rip the neck of her beautiful white dress with its red rose trim with her grasping hands.

Lucha, her sister-in-law, had been married by age sixteen. And she was going on 28 and no one had ever asked to marry her. She hated Lucha, who hadn't been a *señorita* when she married her brother

Antonio. Everyone knew they had fooled around up on the *monte*. And if she had fooled around with Antonio, who else had she fooled around with? An idea came into Lucy's head. An idea that would both serve as the excuse for her absence and get back at her envied sister-in-law.

◯

It was almost midnight when Lucy returned to the house. She knew her brothers would be angry and worried, but she had a plan.

She had almost opened the lock with her key when Mundo flung it open, dragged her inside, and raised his hand to strike her. She burst into tears, "Mi *hermano*, my brother, my poor brother," she sobbed.

Mundo stopped. "Who?"

"My poor brother Antonio," Lucy wailed. Antonio wasn't there. He had walked once more up to the bus stop where Lucy usually got off when she returned from work to see if she had arrived.

That could only mean one thing. "Lucha?" Mundo asked. At that moment Antonio walked in the door, but Lucy pretended not to know he was there. "Yes," Lucy sobbed. "Some days ago. A man. He jumped out the front window."

"*Pinche perra*, I never trusted you." Antonio shouted and grabbed Lucha, who looked unbelievingly at Lucy, and threw her against the wall. Then he began slapping her again and again, saying, "*Pinche puta. Pinche hija de tu chingada madre.*" Then "*pinche puta*," over and over again. Nicolás woke up at that point, and ran out of the back bedroom, stopping Antonio, who at first threatened to hit him as well. Lucha's mouth was bleeding, and drops of blood fell from a nostril. Mundo stood in the corner of the house. He had not stopped his brother. If Petra had been unfaithful to him, he would kill her.

"It's not true, Antonio," Lucha sobbed.

Antonio raised his hand again. "Are you calling my dearest sister a liar?" he demanded.

"But it's not true, Antonio." Lucha cried.

He lifted his hand once again, as though to hit her. "You weren't hard to take up to the *monte* before we were married," he said cruelly.

Then Antonio turned and picked up his *tejana*, nodded at Mundo. They left the house.

O

The Guadalajara Bar on Olympic Boulevard was sizzling this Sunday night, as it was most weekend night. Girls from Mexico and El Salvador adorned the white plastic chairs set around the aluminum tables. A band played in the back, on a slightly lifted, cement block stage. They were playing Ramón Ayala's *Tragos de Amargo Liquor,* when Antonio and Mundo entered.

Mundo and Antonio had often come here to dance before Lucha arrived. Now Mundo and some of the boys from Apartment 25 came occasionally. When the waitress came over, Antonio grabbed a piece of her backside, and said "Two Dos Xes." He swilled down the beer, saying nothing, as Mundo looked around the room. Then he asked one of the barmaids to dance.

Mundo began eyeing a barmaid named Marí who he had danced with a number of times. She reminded him of his sister Lucy, so innocent, so open. He nodded, smiled, and she got up, came over to the table and sat down. Mundo ordered her a beer, knowing by now that it was nothing more than strong tea, but not caring. "I'll have a Dos Xes," too, she surprised him by saying. She got up to get it. When she returned she took a sip, then Mundo asked her to dance. Marí felt good in his arms.

Antonio signaled to him that he was leaving, which surprised Mundo. "*Voy por allá,*" Antonio pointed to the hotel across the street. It was the hotel where the customers took the bargirls. Antonio exited with the bargirl and headed toward the hotel.

"We could go too," Marí suggested to Mundo. Mundo had been unfaithful to Petra only twice. Once when he went to a Los Tigres del Norte concert downtown, and danced with a Mexican-American woman who had smuggled in a bottle of rum, and who, after they were both quite drunk, took him to the backseat of her car, parked outside of the stadium. Once when he had gone to a bar near Pico-Union with some of the boys from Apartment 25, gotten very drunk, and spent the night with an older woman from El Salvador. He had never sought out a prostitute, but tonight confused him. Lucha had brought a man to the house. Lucy said so. Lucy always told the truth when she cried. Lucy had disappeared for two days. He was still angry about that, but forgave her. How could she stay in a house where her brother's wife was bringing men? And then, Petra wanted him to return to the *rancho*, to stay, but there was no way to earn money there. His son, Benjamin was growing meanwhile, and he was not there, he was not a real father.

They went to sit at the table, and Mundo had a second beer, then a third, saying little, staring at the dancers, the band, the men at the other tables who were becoming progressively drunk. "O.K.", he said to Mari, "Let's go."

Eleven: **From L.A. To New York**

From L.A. to New York,
        Cadiz, Marseilles,
                Frankfort, London…

you see them
             on buses
heads bobbing
             with fatigue
as the ride
             one hour or more
                              each way

to jobs
        in garment shops
        in electronics factories
        in meatpacking plants
        in old people's homes
        in construction cleanup
        mopping hospital rooms
        making hospital beds
        as domestic servants
        as busboys
        as dishwashers
        as fast food cooks and waiters
        as fishermen and janitors

sometimes they work a twelve-hour day

then they return
             on buses
heads bobbing
             with fatigue
as they ride
             one hour or more
                    each way
each with   invisible   hidden   secret   lives

to the ghettos where they live
            in apartments
            with leaky pipes
            radiators not working in winter
            plumbing not worth the metal
            cracked windows
            creaking floors
            cockroaches
            rats

from jobs
            people
say
                                    they are robbing
            from citizens
                        say
            they don't pay enough taxes
            for all the services they use
                        say
            they come in   invade
            cross borders   illegally
            cause the economy
            to be the way it is
                        say
            everything that's going wrong
            well   it's all their fault

you see them
                        on buses
heads bobbing
                        with fatigue
as they ride
                        one hour or more
                                                each way

far from home

                        from some foreign place

where they left loved ones

to look for
                jobs at minimum wage
                jobs no one wants
                jobs that barely pay
                        the rent
                        if you live
                        with
                        just one wage earner
                dirty jobs
                        without prestige
                dangerous jobs
                        without a future

they're stealing them all

you see them
                        on buses
heads bobbing
                        with fatigue
as they ride
                        one hour or more
                                                each way
mexicans and el salvadoreans in los angeles
dominicans and haitians in new york
morrocans in cadiz
west africans in marseilles
turks in frankfort
west indians in london
chinese, pakistanis, guatemalans, filipinos, vietnamese,
hondurans, thais

                persons   displaced by

                        colonialism
                                or
                        imperialism

or

wars

and

struggles

civil   or otherwise

you see them

on buses…

An earlier version was published in *Struggle*, 1993, Vol.9, No.2, pp. 2-4.

Twelve: **Lucha Letter**

June 1988
West Los Angeles

My dearest Mamá

I hope this letter finds you and my sister Bertha and my brother Rogelio in good health, as these are my desires. Mamá I know I should not write you the following because a daughter does not share such things with her mother and a good woman with any woman, but I must tell you, you are so far away and may not understand if I don't tell you because no one can tell you my story but me. And it helps me to write this all down though I don't know if I will send this letter to you, if you will ever read it, but I will write it all down.

I want to tell you about what happened because there were many witnesses from the rancho both from our family and the family of my husband Antonio and if you do not hear it from me you will hear it from one of them or their family and it will bother you more, hurt you more, because it has to do with the wellbeing of your oldest grandchild, my son Miguelito.

More than a year ago Lucy my sister-in-law made my husband Antonio angry with me. She pretended she had seen me with another man just to cover up her own badness when she ran away for a weekend, although no one knows where she went, but she is man crazy, always swishing around in high heels and more recently in sleeveless dresses. Do not tell anyone I told you about my sister-in-law Lucy or it will go worse for me with my husband Antonio and his brothers, my brothers-in-law, but that is what happened. My husband Antonio became furious with me because my sister-in-law Lucy lied and told him she had seen me with another man in our house, and that is why she went away she said, because she was not living in a respectful house, and my husband Antonio started going to the bars, with my brother-in-law Mundo, and seeing other women. Tell Mundo's wife Petra she must come because they are all going out to the bars and there are many loose women in the bars who go with anyone even if he is married besides the women of the bad life who take money from anyone and she may end up like my cousin by marriage Luís's wife, sharing her husband and his earnings, even though my cousin by marriage Luís says his woman here does not ask him for money because she earns her own. That hurt me, my husband Antonio

*began going to the bars with some of the other muchachos and breaking
our wedding vows with other women who are prostitutas and who I heard
my sister-in-law Gabriela's husband say they take to a hotel near the bar
where they go, and spend even more money that we need at home, but
the worst was yet to come.*

*This is what happened. It happened during a party for my son
Miguelito's 10th birthday when my husband Antonio got very drunk
and started calling me a damned whore, a pinche puta, yes in front of
everyone including my comadre Elena and my compadre Hilario, even
though I have never been with any man other than him and never wear
sleeveless blouses or short skirts, usually I wear pants and always when
I go to work, unlike my sister-in-law Lucy who always wear skirts and
dresses and some of them short and without sleeves and usually some
shade of red which she prefers, and high heels even to work, while I wear
tans and browns and whites and tennis shoes that do not call so much
attention to myself and of course blue jeans. Well my husband Antonio
was drunk and cursing me and calling me a whore and he had a beer in
his hand which he was drinking fast and looking at me and swearing, then
he came after me with the beer bottle upraised, trying to hit me, but my
son Miguelito put himself between us, and when my husband Antonio
tried to hit me with the beer bottle, my son Miguelito pushed me back,
and my husband Antonio missed me and hit Miguelito a hard blow on
his little head. And my son Miguelito bled all over the floor, all over the
grey rug, and all over me, there are still stains on the rug, my husband
Antonio shouting it was my fault for being a puta, that it had been my
fault for being a pinche puta that he had hit my son Miguelito, until my
cousin by marriage Luís and my compadre Hilario took him into the
bedroom and tried to calm him down, while my brother-in-law Mundo
who believes everything his sister Lucy says, just looked on, except my
brother-in-law Mundo did go for a cloth to clean up Miguelito's little face
which was filled with blood from the wound on his little head.*

*Meanwhile my son Miguelito kept bleeding, bleeding through his
chestnut brown hair, bleeding over everything but not crying, just
stunned and silent because his father, my husband, had hit him such a
blow. We had to take him to the emergency in the hospital where they
put in 11 stitches, this after shaving most of the hair off his little head.
My poor little soccer ball head. And the police came to the hospital, also
Luís and his wife here in Los Angeles because she speaks some English
even though she's from El Salvador, but she finished high school there so*

that's probably how she learned it, in any case she speaks more English than my husband Antonio and I do, or Mundo or Nicolás or Luís or my compadres, although I can say "please" and "thank you" and some other small words and I understand when my patronas tell me to wash or clean something. And the police questioned every one of us, there was my husband Antonio, my brother-in-law Mundo and my cousin by marriage Luís and his wife in Los Angeles, her name is Sara, Lucy didn't come although she wanted to but there was no room in the car so she went home with my sister in law Gabriela and her husband Oníforo where she is staying now. They questioned every one of us because they were going to put whoever did it in jail, but we didn't want my husband Antonio to go to jail because without him how could we pay the rent and the food and everything? Besides he would come out of jail even meaner and hit us again for having told them what happened. So we agreed to a story that we were walking along Sawtelle and a drunk came out of Cozy Corner, where Rosario and Alvaro used to live, and tried to hit my husband Antonio with a beer bottle but missed and hit my son Miguelito instead. But Sara, my cousin by marriage Luís's wife, almost gave in to the police, she kept hesitating and looking down then looking over to my son Miguelito then looking at me, because they told her it was a crime, it was child abuse, and whoever did it should go to jail and if it happened again they would take my son Miguelito away from us. But she held up and stuck to our story. And I was afraid they would want to see where we live because they took down our address, and if they came to where we live they would find out what happened because of the blood and broken glass all over the rug. They didn't believe what we told them you see, but we all stuck to the story, though Sara was very nervous, and my husband Antonio was drunk and didn't repent at all, he just stayed silent in front of the police, but didn't repent at all, not even the next day when he was sober but with a hangover, only telling me that it was my fault for being a whore, that if I hadn't been a whore, it would never have happened, and I, who never cry, cried and cried all day the day after he hit my Miguelito over his little head, my Miguelito who never cried but walked around stunned and silent for several days, not believing his Papá had hit him. And we had bought my Miguelito a big birthday cake but while we were away at the hospital the roaches got in it, and we were never able to eat any of it, though it cost quite a bit of money.

I was glad my brother Edgar had gone, he is still in Chicago as you know, because he might have fought with my husband Antonio and nothing good would have come of it. I have decided to leave him, Mamá, even though I know you put up with terrible things with my Papá and stayed but where would you have gone with the five children you had until my littlest brother died and we remained only four. I am just waiting to receive my amnesty papers, Mamá, they should be here within the next two weeks or so. Maybe I will go to stay with my Aunt Lidia in Chicago where my brother Edgar is now. Because if I move to my cousin Esther's in Inglewood which is only about 20 or 30 kilometers from here, my husband Antonio will get drunk and take me back by force, because I am his wife and he can do anything with me he pleases, that's what men think, as you know. I will save my money from selling tamales for the airfare, though it will be hard because my sister-in-law Lucy wants to help me make them and sell them for half the money. And I can't tell her no because my husband Antonio would be angrier and say that I only want to go to the park to flirt with men though it is his sister Lucy who likes to flirt with men in her red dresses and high heels while I wear blue jeans and western shirts and cowboy boots my husband Antonio bought me one time when I go on Sundays to sell tamales in the park. But that is what he thinks of me after Lucy told him she saw me with another man. And I had so many hopes Mamá when my husband Antonio brought me across even though when he got drunk on the rancho he would often talk roughly to me but never as bad as this.

It is necessary that my air fare will have to come from selling tamales since almost all I earn from cleaning houses goes into clothing and food and paying for my son Miguelito's clothes and school supplies, and now to help pay the rent, though my husband Antonio and my brother in law Mundo and my cousin by marriage Nicolás are good about paying the rent, though since my brother Edgar left it is harder on them so I pay my part. And then my cousin by marriage Nicolás is sometimes staying with my husband's uncle Ignacio in the apartments where the other boys from the rancho live and maybe he will move to stay there, especially since he gets gloomy when my husband Antonio curses me or talks badly to me. But anyway I will take my son Miguelito and go, if God wills it, though I don't know if God will will it since my husband Antonio and I married in church and supposedly I must cleave to him for life, come what may, but he is so mean and does not respect me as a husband should according to our vows. And I know you stayed with my Papá even though he mistreated you, until the day he was thrown from the horse and killed, but I am afraid for my brave little son Miguelito, who didn't cry even

*when they put the stitches in and walked around without talking for days
thereafter even though he is usually very talkative, like me, who have also
stopped talking a lot when my husband Antonio is around, in case he
finds fault with what I say and often curses me for little things like if the
tortillas are not hot enough when I serve dinner or if I have failed to wash
one of the shirts he wants to put on that day. May the Virgin protect us,
and may the Virgin protect my Mamá and my brothers and sister, as these
are my wishes for us.*

Your daughter Lucha who may never send this letter to you.

Thirteen: **Nicolás and Ignacio**

I. 1985

Mundo's father and Nicolás's father had married sisters. And these sisters had a brother, Ignacio, who was uncle to them both. But Nicolás and his *tío* Ignacio had more in common than other members of the family who migrated to Los Angeles. First, they never got a steady job that lasted more than a few months. For *tío* Ignacio this was partially because, when he was away from his wife he drank too much, and he drank daily. Sometimes he missed work and after he did so a number of times he was fired. For Nicolás it had been the luck of the draw—the jobs he picked up on Sawtelle Boulevand simply did not last more than a few days, a few weeks, or a few months. Second, Nicolás and Ignacio shared the fact that they were deeply in love with their wives, and hated to be separated from them. This meant that they traveled back to the *rancho* every few months. It also meant that they could not afford to pay *coyotes* for their trips back.

Nicolás had once thought of bringing Miranda over to the United States so he wouldn't have to spend so much money going back and forth, but after she got pregnant for the third time, they gave up the idea. In any case he didn't want to share his home with her with anyone else, but there was no way he could afford to rent a place for them alone. So he went back to visit a lot. Although at first they crossed the border in Tecate where the other boys from the *rancho* did, with the aid of a *coyote*, because the cost of *coyotes* was immense, Nicolás and Ignacio learned to cross the border without one. They crossed sometimes from San Luis Río Colorado, Sonora, walked to Yuma, Arizona and there jumped a train to Los Angeles or vicinity. It was vicinity which made it difficult for Mundo and Antonio and Luís to know where they were, where they should pick them up, now that Antonio had a pick-up.

"We're in Fontana," Nicolás said on one phone call to Mundo. "Will you come and get us? We don't have money for the bus."

"Where in Fontana?" Mundo asked, unsure even of where Fontana was.

"At the hamburger place."

It was about seven in the evening when the call came through and Mundo and Antonio got into Antonio's old Ford pick-up and drove the hour and a half to two hours out to Fontana. They exited the freeway and began driving up and down the main street looking for "the hamburger place." They came to a plaza in the center of town and there were all the chains of hamburger places they had ever seen in Los Angeles, a few streets away from one another. They checked them out, walking from one to another, entered into a world of teenagers laughing and talking and wearing shorts, and felt strange. But they found no Nicolás or Ignacio, and after awhile of sitting in the pick-up in the plaza, watching people go by they went back to Los Angeles, getting there about 1 a.m., to wait by the phone.

Less than half an hour after they arrived, Nicolás called again. "Why didn't you pick us up?" he asked.

Mundo answered, somewhat miffed, "We went to every hamburger place in Fontana. There were loads of them. You weren't in any one."

"We still are at the hamburger place, but it closed down two hours ago. We're out in front."

"Which damned hamburger place?," Mundo inquired.

"The one near the train station," Nicolás replied. "Right after you get off the freeway."

That one they hadn't been to, hadn't known about, they had only been to the hamburger places downtown. So they got into the pick-up again, Antonio and Mundo, and drove the one and a half to two hours back to Fontana. When they got off the freeway and passed the railroad tracks they started looking. Antonio pulled up to the gas station with the twenty-four hour convenience store to fill up the tank and just then cousin Nicolás and uncle Ignacio walked out of it with a cup of coffee each.

"We figured we'd find you when you drove off the freeway," Nicolás explained as they climbed in the back of the pick-up.

They often came this way, crossing in San Luís Río Colorado, walking to Yuma, and then jumping a train. Then Miranda's aunt Lilia, who had moved to Mexicali more than 35 years ago, came back to her *rancho* on the occasion of her father's death and visited relatives in the surrounding *ranchos* at the same time. She had invited her sister, who lived in Santa Rosa, and her sister's children to come and visit anytime they liked. Miranda told Nicolás that her *tía* Lilia and *tío* Juan would be able to orient them to that city and that Lilia had told her that there were ways of crossing from Mexicali without having to use a *coyote*.

Just climb the fence separating Mexicali from Calexico and walk a few blocks to the Greyhound Station. Tickets to Los Angeles were only about 12 dollars and three buses went each day.

So this time Nicolás and Ignacio were going to try to cross in Mexicali, staying with Nicolás's wife's aunt until they were able to do so.

O

When they got off at the bus station in Mexicali they asked an ice cream vendor how to get to Colonia Popular and decided to walk the 6 kilometers or so, partially because they were unsure what bust to take and partially because they wanted to save money. Carrying their small backpacks containing a change of clothes and a bottle of water, they walked east on Avenida Independencia and when they got to Boulevard Benito Juárez they turned south. They walked a few blocks past the university and decided to ask directions again, this time from a newspaper vendor who stood on the crossway selling to drivers in the passing cars. It turned out he lived in Colonia Popular and he said that if they would help him sell his last several dozen newspapers, he would take them there, it was only about two kilometers further on. So when the traffic lights turned red the three went to the stopped cars, offering their passengers *La Voz de la Frontera*.

Ernesto, the newspaper vendor, knew Juan and Lilia and their family. One of their sons—Román—was his age, fifteen, and they sometimes hung out together. Ernesto said everyone knew everyone else in the *colonia*, it was a small *colonia*, established only three years ago, but now they had electricity. All of the families had to get together to stage the invasion, then to regularize the lots with the government, then to pressure for electricity. They didn't have potable water yet though. People put barrels outside their houses, and a water truck came around to fill them. His eldest brother, Marcelo, drove one of them, the *pipa*. "And can you drink it?" *tío* Ignacio wanted to know. No, Ernesto explained, another truck came around with water in blue plastic bottles. Only that could be drunk, unless you wanted to become very sick.

They got to Lilia's and Juan's house about 6:30. It was a two-room house made of recycled wooden planks, with dirt floors, much like Nicolás's and Miranda's house on the *rancho*, but with two rooms instead of one and less land around it. Juan was asleep. Lilia, a talkative woman, explained that he had to go to work in a few hours. He worked as a night watchman for a truck stop down the highway. He had taken that job in his mid-fifties because it came with social security and after ten years he would get a pension. After leaving Zacatecas he had worked at odd jobs, whether picking broccoli or lettuce or as a car mechanic's assistant or as a brick maker's helper sometimes in the Imperial Valley and sometimes in Mexicali. But those jobs did not come with *seguro* with its package of medical benefits.

Lilia took Nicolás and *tío* Ignacio next door to meet her second eldest son, Fernando, and his wife Luz, who was almost six months pregnant. It turned out Fernando had been born in Brawley, California during the two years Lilia and Juan had lived there, both jumping the downtown fence separating Mexicali from Calexico. They had crossed with their eldest and only child, a boy then three years old, and joined a friend of Juan's who had a green card. Fernando, at thirty, had become the foreman for a lettuce company, after working in the Imperial Valley fields, and sometimes in Salinas, for fourteen years. He was the only one of his siblings who could cross to work legally, having been born a U.S. citizen, but he was planning to give his youngest brother Román, now 15, a job in the lettuce fields next year.

Fernando and Nicolás were near the same age and hit it off well. He asked Nicolás and Ignacio what work they had done in Los Angeles. Construction cleanup, painting houses, gardener's helper, loading and unloading trucks. Nicolás's longest job had been cleaning a gym, Ignacio's as a cook's helper in a Chinese restaurant. Both had lost those jobs when they returned to Santa Martha for a month.

Fernando suggested they come to work for him in the lettuce fields. It was harvest time in the Imperial Valley and the lettuce cutting would continue until the end of March. From early April to early November he would take his crew to Salinas. Same company, same work. Two of his workers, brothers who lived in Colonia Popular, had had to go back to their *rancho* in Sinaloa because of some family problems just last week, so he had openings.

Nicolás and Ignacio were interested, so Fernando told them what they would have to do. They would have to cross through a hole in the fence in a *colonia* called Baja California. From the hole they would see a large supermarket and on the other side of the supermarket ran West 2nd Street. They should take West 2nd Street two blocks east to

Imperial Avenue, then turn north, and meet him at the Kentucky Fried Chicken parking lot. That's where he picked up his workers to take them out to the fields. They should be there between 5 and 5:15, since he left for the fields at 5:30. They had to start picking at 6 a.m. He could take them back across the border to the *colonia* after they finished work—anytime between 4 and 6 p.m.—because going south into Mexico they wouldn't be checked for documents by the U.S. *migra*. The pay would be 4 dollars an hour if they wanted to keep the job and worked well.

They could catch a ride to Colonia Baja California with a young widow who lived three streets over. She took other field hands to the hole in the fence every morning, and had taken the brothers from Sinaloa. She left the *colonia* at 3:30 a.m. and charged 6 dollars each person each day.

Fernando offered to take them over to meet her, but it was late and the bus ride to Mexicali had taken 38 hours, so Nicolás and Ignacio asked Fernando to let them think about it for a day, but probably yes, and tomorrow evening he could take them to meet the widow.

Both Miranda's *tía* Lilia and Miranda's cousin Fernando offered Nicolás and Ignacio a place to stay, Lilia in her kitchen, and Fernando and Luz in the half-finished, unroofed second bedroom they were putting up as part of the brick house they were building—one of the few in the *colonia* made of such substantial materials, but still with dirt floors. They ended up staying with Fernando, as it would be easier in terms of when the family woke up if they stayed to work with him. Lilia, however, insisted on lending each a blanket, saying that these months were cold in Mexicali—sometimes the puddles of water, or even the barrels of water had a slim cake of ice on them early in the morning.

O

The next day Nicolás and Ignacio had breakfast with Lilia and Juan and their son Román and their daughter-in-law, Luz. Lilia had arisen before 6 a.m. to fry potatoes and beans, to make a salsa of tomatoes, chilis and onions, and to heat the corn tortillas. Juan came home from his job as night watchman by 6:30 and Román had to leave a little before 8 to walk the three blocks over and one block up to José's car body shop, where he worked as an apprentice-helper.

Nicolás and *tío* Ignacio walked with Román to the body shop, set up under a tarpaulin on the lot where José lived, watched him removing the paint from an old Chevrolet. After awhile they left to walk around the *colonia*, which they found to be five blocks wide and two blocks deep. A broad canyon of land separated Colonia Popular from a nearby working-class sites-and services *fraccionamiento*. At least that is what Constantino, and old man they met along the way had told them—that it was a *colonia* of the better-off. Constantino also told them that the municipality was going to turn the canyon into the next city dump, infill it with layers of garbage. The old man was happy about that because he would be able to collect metals and other stuff for resale to the junk dealers. Maybe even find some new clothes, cast off by people who had more money than he had. He would be a garbage picker now, but the dump was way out near the airport and he had no way to get there. It took two hours and three buses to reach the dump, and even then you had to walk two kilometers, and how was he going to carry his pickings back? Don Juan on the corner had a pick-up but his wife and three children went along to pick, and together they filled the truck up with the cardboard they recycled in the course of the day. There was no room for him. So he walked along the highway and picked up aluminum cans that drivers threw out of their windows.

After talking for awhile Nicolás and Ignacio took leave of the old man and walked up another street. They noticed that there will some empty lots scattered around the *colonia*. They talked about cutting lettuce. Four dollars an hour was more than they usually got in Los Angeles. Even employers who paid the minimum daily wage usually gave them only 30 dollars a day, and many paid less than the minimum. Here they were guaranteed at least that, and probably more, as Fernando had told them that most often they worked ten hours a day. So they would try it. In Los Angeles they had lived 12 to 15 to a studio apartment off Butler. That meant they were never lonely, but it was also stressful and sometimes harsh words were spoken. Here they had their own room—if they were welcome. And it looked like either Miranda's *tía* Lilia or Fernando's wife Luz would do the cooking. They would give them at least two days pay for their board and room. That is what they did in Los Angeles. But there they also had to do the cooking, alternating among themselves. They agreed that it seemed a good deal. Just so the *migra* didn't catch them when they went through the hole in the fence. Fernando had told them the *migra* knew about

the hole but also knew the local farmers needed workers, so did not
patrol there early in the mornings. If they went to Los Angeles they
would somehow have to pass through the immigration checkpoints San
Clemente or Temescula. Staying was easier.

After awhile they went back to José's body shop. José put them to
work washing two cars, for which he gave them the equivalent of 2
dollars each.

When Fernando got back from work, about 6 p.m., Nicolás and
Ignacio told him that they were thinking about working in the lettuce
fields, but didn't want to impose on him and Luz for a place to stay.
Fernando told them they were in-laws—husband and *tío político* of his
cousin Miranda, and they could stay as long as they liked. He needed
two more men on his crew since the brothers from Sinaloa had gone
back south.

Fernando took them over to meet the widow Julia and explained
to her that Nicolás and Ignacio would need a ride to the hole in the
fence, with her other passengers. Julia told Nicolás and Ignacio that
it cost 6 dollars a day. She was usually paid for the week in advance,
every Monday morning, but she would trust them for this week until
they were paid on Saturday for their work from tomorrow on. Julia told
them they should be at the small *tienda* near the entrance to the *colonia*
around 3 a.m. She left for the border at 3:30. It would take her almost
an hour to get them to the fence in Colonia Baja California.

◯

Fernando got them up a little before 3 next morning, a Thursday.
They left without breakfast and walked the two blocks to the *tiendita*.
Two men and a woman joined them for the ride. The two young
men, Alberto and Edelberto were brothers, originally from a *rancho*
in Jalisco, and worked in the broccoli with a brother-in-law, husband
of their eldest sister. Both their sister and their parents had lots in the
colonia. The woman, from Sinaloa, crossed to work six days a week
cleaning a house and caring for children in El Centro. The bus from
Calexico to where the family lived took more than an hour, and then
there was waiting time, so to get to her job that started at 7:30, she had
to cross the border by 5:30. She had had a border crossing card when
she first found the job, but one day in downtown Mexicali, as she was
getting on a bus to come back to the *colonia*, a man had put his hand

in her purse and robbed her wallet. What made her most angry was
that there was a policeman no more than 10 meters away. When she
pointed out the man who had stolen her wallet and asked him to stop
the their, he merely looked at her, then told her she would have to
go to police headquarters, more than 4 kilometers away, to report the
robo. When she applied for a new border crossing card it was denied,
on the ground that she had no formal job in Mexicali, nor was she
supported by a husband, since she was single. She had been working at
a *maquiladora* when she applied the first time, and this had satisfied the
migra. In any case, for almost 9 months now, she had crossed to work in
El Centro through the hole. Just once every two weeks or so, the *migra*
would be sitting on the other side of the fence near the hole, in their
lime green jeeps or vans, and then no one could cross at that spot.

O

They crossed uneventfully in the still dark morning, and walked
across a dirt track and then an empty field toward the supermarket.
Alberto told them that he and his brother were going to a diner almost
across Imperial Boulevard from Kentucky Fried Chicken, so he could
show them the way. It was in the parking lot of the diner that his
foreman picked he and his brother up.

The streets were almost empty at this hour. Only farm workers
huddled in groups along various pick-up spots on East Second Avenue
and on Imperial. There were at least twenty other men and two
women at the Kentucky Fried Chicken parking lot when Nicolás and
tío Ignacio got there. Nicolás and Ignacio kept to the edges of the
various small groups that had formed. At 5:17 Fernando arrived in the
fourteen passenger white Chevrolet van that had been parked in front
of his house in Colonia Popular. His crew slowly climbed in, most with
lettuce knives on their belts, and Nicolás and Ignacio followed them.
Fernando drove up Imperial Boulevard to highway 98 then turned east
toward Yuma, Arizona.

O

Nicolás and his *tío* Ignacio continued to work cutting lettuce for the
next few months. The first two weeks had been the worst, backs aching

from bending, knees hurting from bending, first to the left to cut a head of lettuce, then to the right to do the same, one step forward, then again to the left and again to the right. This for from 8 to 10 hours a day. But they had gotten used to it. With their first full week's salary they bought some rubber boots for working in the fields, their own lettuce knives, paid off their 9 day debt to the widow Julia, and gave 40 dollars each to Luz for their board and room. Luz did not want to accept the money at first, but Ignacio said that it would help Fernando to build the house faster. At that she gave in. Fernando brought them lunch every day, 3 or 4 small *burritos* made by Luz and filled with beans and franks, or potatoes and chorizo or eggs and bologna or whatever was left over from the previous evening's meal. Almost every two weeks a lime green jeep would drive up the track on the Calexico side of the hole, then lurk there. On those days they could not cross, so Ignacio and Nicolás, escorted by Alberto and Edelberto would roam around Mexicali, down town, the Civic Center, and sometimes they would go to a movie. Nicolás found it interesting that while in Santa Monica and downtown Los Angeles they saw Mexican movies, here in Mexicali most were American movies. Ignacio and Nicolás learned the bus route from down town and from the Civic Center—two blocks over from where they had gotten off the bus to Mexicali—back to the *colonia*. Still, sometimes the four of them would walk the 6 or so kilometers back to the *colonia*.

Saturday nights Fernando would buy a case of liter bottles of Tecate and they would sit around a fire he had built at the front of the lot. Román would come and ask a multitude of questions. He was especially interested in the story of Ignacio's working in a Chinese restaurant. There were more than thirty Chinese restaurants in Mexicali, he told them, and he had been to three of them when he delivered sodas for the Coca Cola company, but most of the waiters and the cooks had been Chinese or half-Chinese. He finally got Ignacio to talking, something that usually happened only after Ignacio had downed a couple of beers. And this particular Saturday, he had downed three.

O

"When I was in Los Angeles I got short time work by standing on Sawtelle every morning, being employed by the day, by the week and sometimes for months, and then let go when the job was over. One day I had no luck and I walked down to the Japanese nursery that sometimes gave me work for a few hours, but there was no luck there either. I walked north on Sawtelle, passing the second hand store, then turned right, walking through the playing field where sometimes the boys got together to play baseball or soccer, and continued walking over to Westwood Boulevard, then north again."

"There was a Chinese man standing in front of a small take-out Chinese food restaurant and watching me, and watching me, and I felt rather strange about being watched so intently, but I nodded and said "*Buenos días,*" expecting no reply. But to my surprise the man answered me saying "*Buenos días.*" I was pretty surprised and I stopped, somewhat stunned, because I had never talked to a Chinese person before.

"*Usted habla español?*" I asked."

"Sure, the man replied. My father and mother lived in Mexicali, immigrated here in 1966. My great-grandfather went when he was very young to pick cotton in the Mexicali Valley. Before the Mexican Revolution."

I held out my hand, "Ignacio Trejo Contreras, para sevirle."

"Luis Chong Cinco, *para servirle,*" the man replied. "Do you know anybody who is looking for work?"

"What kind of work?" I asked.

"I need a cook's helper for the restaurant."

"Chinese food?"

"Yes," Luis Chang Cinco said, "You just have to cut up meat and vegetables, sometimes cook some rice. But it isn't hard. I pay 3.50 dollars an hour."

"Well, I make rice and beans and pork in *mole burritos* for the boys where I live on my turn," I said after I thought about it for a moment. "So why not?"

"Can you begin tomorrow, 12 p.m. to 10 p.m.?"

"And that is how it was that I came to be a cook's helper in a Chinese restaurant and get to know how to prepare Chinese food."

Román asked Nicolás if he had tried Ignacio's Chinese cooking. Nicolás replied: "My *tío* often brought Chinese food back to the boys in the apartment and several times on his turn made chicken with cashews and chilis and brocolli and beef and once even made sweet and sour pork for us. It was great."

"But" Ignacio, continued "I had a problem. I wanted my wife to try Chinese food. Although the men cook for themselves when they

are without women in the United States, and any kind of work is
honorable, it would not do for men to cook back on the *rancho*. My
wife wouldn't even let me in the kitchen to heat a tortilla! I could try
to tell her how to do it, but I didn't want to admit I was working as a
cook. And she would resist me telling her how to cook anything, unless
she had tried it first."

Luz loved the story, saying, yes, that is the way it is back on the
rancho. But she had taught all of her four children, two boys, two girls,
how to cook—in case the boys were ever alone or their wives were
pregnant and needed a hand. There were not the same amount of
relatives one could call on here, as back on the *ranchos*, she pointed
out. Luz, who was six months pregnant said that if she had a boy she
would teach him to cook too.

Fernando asked if Ignacio's wife had ever tried his Chinese cooking.
"Well, yes," Ignacio admitted. "I went into Fresnillo, my wife thought
on business, and I bought the cabbage and ginger for the twice-cooked
pork. There wasn't any broccoli to make broccoli and beef so I bought
some cashews and *chiles de arbol* to make kung pao chicken. I bought
the pork and the chicken back on the *rancho*. Then I went over to
my little sister's house and started cooking up a storm. She thought it
was very funny. Then I left some for my sister and took the rest over
to my wife. At first I said it was made by my sister. But then there was
the question how would my sister, who had never eaten Chinese food,
know how to cook it. When it finally came out that I had made it my
wife found it very funny and said I could cook once a week if I wanted
to. She wanted me to show her how to make it. Wasn't angry at all.
Didn't put me down at all."

◯

After the lettuce cutting was over in the Imperial Valley Nicolás
and Ignacio decided to go back to the *rancho* rather than trying
to make it up to Salinas. They had been away from their wives
for more than three months in any case. Both wanted to see them
again. And Fernando would be at risk if he took them up in the
van. If the *migra* stopped him and found out he had undocumented
workers as passengers, they might confiscate Fernando's only means
of transportation. They could take the bus up, but there were many
immigration check points along the way, not just San Clemente or

Temescula, but others north of Los Angeles. And it was well known that if the immigration check points were open, the *migra* boarded the buses and checked the papers of all of those who looked Mexican.

Nicolás and Ignacio had each saved over a thousand dollars on this trip. Nicolás gave most of it to Miranda, who bought two young goats with part of it. Ignacio also gave his wife the biggest portion. She had wanted to have glass windows put in the house, and the money would enable her to do so. In mid-May they returned to Mexicali then one early morning walked through the hole and caught a bus to Los Angeles. The trip was uneventful. The immigration check point in Temescula was closed.

For the next two years, every January through March, they stayed with Fernando and Luz in Mexicali and worked in the lettuce fields across the border

II. 1986-87

In 1986 the Immigration Control and Reform Act (IRCA) was passed. Its Special Agricultural Worker provisions included one that bestowed amnesty on anyone who had worked in the agricultural fields for more than 90 days in the previous year. Fernando got letters from the company affirming that Nicolás and Ignacio had been among his work crew in 1985 and then again in 1986. So did Nicolás and Ignacio receive amnesty.

Another provision of the law was that anyone who had lived in the United States since January 1, 1982 and could prove it, would also get amnesty as Legally Authorized Workers (LAW).

Antonio, as well as Luís, his cousin, had arrived together in Los Angeles, in 1979. Antonio had rental receipts to prove it. Lucha had followed him in 1983. She had telephone receipts to prove it and one of her *patronas* had written a letter saying Lucha had worked for her since December 1980. The guards wrote Mundo a letter saying that he had been employed there since 1981. Luís had worked as a gardener for several house owners in a nearby gated community, and they gave him letters saying so. Edgar had no proof of anything, nor did Lucy, nor Gabriela and her husband. They had arrived after the cut-off date. Gabriela and her husband did have a daughter born in 1986 in Los Angeles County Hospital.

III. 1988

Nicolás and Ignacio had noticed, when they stayed with Fernando and Luz, that there were still empty lots in the *colonia*, and also that many of the original invaders were selling their lots. It was possible to buy a lot for as little as 600 dollars. They saved more than that during their three months in the Imperial Valley lettuce fields. Nicolás wondered whether leaving the *rancho* to come to live in Mexicali would be alright with Miranda.

On one visit home after getting his amnesty card, he said "Miranda, let's move to Mexicali."

"Mexicali?" she replied in an awed way.

"There are lots in the Colonia where your Aunt Lilia and cousin Fernando live. I could buy one with three months work. I can work across the border, and always be home at night. Except for a few months when I would have to work in Salinas. We could build our house there bit by bit, as the other *colonos* did."

Miranda stood resting on one leg, twisting a cleaning rag in her hands, waiting for more. To leave the *rancho*, when she had never been more than walking distance or a short horse back ride away in her life, except once, after the birth of their first son, when Nicolás had taken her to the church of the *Niño de Atocha* to give thanks. They had stopped in Fresnillo on the way back and walked among the vendors, some of whom sold radio-cassette players that entranced her. She never thought she'd have such a wondrous thing, but Nicolás had a lovely large one, silver colored with flashing lights, nicer than anything they had seen in Fresnillo, and brought it to her the first time he came back from the United States. She played it, not too long, careful of the eight batteries it took to run it. She played it turned low so that it would not wear out so soon, the music of *rancheras* and *corridos* filling the windowless one room adobe house, while she swept the floors or laundered the clothes or made tortillas or played with the children.

"I can get steady work in the fields," Nicolás continued. "And we can build our own little house again. This time with two rooms. Even three. The pay is good and the work is steady. And we won't be apart so much anymore."

She still just stood and looked at him, waiting for more. Her aunt was there. She had someone, even though she would have to leave her sister here. Or maybe her sister could come also some day? The possibilities loomed large. Leave all the known, go to the unknown. But, be with her husband. Have him come home from work every night. She threw the cleaning rag down on the wooden stove top, and rushed to him, "Yes, my little husband. Let us go."

"And we'll have running water in the house," Nicolás said as he held her close to him. "They are going to put in running water this coming year."

And so Miranda and Nicolás and their three children went to join her *tía* in Mexicali, where they stayed for a few months until they got their own lot in the *colonia*, and while Nicolás put aside money for the materials to build their little house, a shabby one perhaps, made out of low quality wood, but with windows, and soon with electricity and a faucet on the lot which saved Miranda from going down, as she did on the *rancho*, to the dam with the wheelbarrow carrying buckets which she filled with the milky, amoeba filled water, and brought back up the hill to their house to wash selves and clothes and dishes, something Nicolás could not help her with while he was away, though he did help her when he was at home, despite the derisive remarks by the men clustered in front of the store drinking beer, about his doing women's work.

Ignacio stayed with Nicolás when he crossed the border, and sometimes Nicolás accompanied him on the bus as far as Indio, and after he bought an old second-hand Dodge, even took him to Los Angeles occasionally. But Ignacio had no heart to start over again in Mexicali. His two decades of work had gone into making his house on the *rancho* beautiful, giving his money to his wife to put in windows, to buy the material for curtains, to plaster the house and paint it bright rose, to put in electricity and lamps and a color television set, to build two more rooms, so that the house was among the biggest in the *rancho* and far more comfortable than the apartment where he lived in Los Angeles. It was too late for him to begin another life.

But things changed for Ignacio, for he now had amnesty too. He could go back and forth to visit his wife whenever he wished. Take a bus from Mexicali or Tijuana to Los Angeles. And not have to worry about paying a *coyote* or sneaking across the border.

Fourteen: **Lucha letter**

Chicago
November 1988

My dearest Mamá,

I hope this letter finds you and my sister Berta and my brother Rogelio well, as these are my desires. I am here in Chicago now with my brother Edgar and my aunt Lidia. As you know, your sister-in-law Lidia is working in a nursing home, and she is going to try to get me a job there. She said the gringa workers leave after a short time because they find it too hard. But it will be just like cleaning houses except that I will also have to change sheets and wash them, but not by hand, in a washing machine. There are washing machines everywhere here, Mamá, in people's houses or in places where they have a lot of them, called laundramats, and you put in some coins to make them work. That is always where I went in Los Angeles to wash clothes. No more hand washing of everything. Someday I will buy you one, now that the house has electricity. I will look for a park here in Chicago to sell tamales on Sundays, as I did in Los Angeles, and every bit of money I earn from selling tamales I'll put away to buy to buy you a washing machine. Now that there is electricity on the rancho. The only problem is that you cannot sell here all year around as you can in Los Angeles. It is so very cold, and there is snow everywhere in the winter. It was snowing the day we arrived, I had never seen snow before, and it was soft and cold and tasted like ice cream before you put the flavor in it, and it stayed and stayed for days turning from soft to ice you could hardly walk on and then into slush that wet your shoes. And my son Miguelito loves to play in it, he made a snowball, several snowballs, the first day here, but his little hands turned red and hurt him when we went back into the apartment, so I have bought him gloves. And the snow comes and goes at least five or six months the year my aunt Lidia told me, and for those months I will not be able to stay out more than two or three hours on Sundays to sell tamales, if that, because the air is so cold sometimes it cuts you like a knife, especially when it is windy. And you need more clothes here, sweaters and jackets and boots and heavy socks and gloves, so I will have to spend some of the money I earn when I get to work to buy them. They have good second-hand stores here, as in Los Angeles, and with the money I saved before I came I have bought some winter clothes for my Miguelito and I and Edgar bought my Miguelito a winter jacket at the Goodwill.

My aunt Lidia is doing well as in my brother Edgar and my Miguelito. My tía Lidia told me something I didn't know, that she would never have married Mario except that he came and robbed her and took her away to a cave for three days, then what could she do since no man would have her after that. And that she left home to come to Chicago as soon as the children were grown, more than 15 years ago, she's going to be 62 now, and has no desire to ever see Mario again, and that she always hated him for what he did to her, even though she was a good wife to him and bore him children, because she had someone she loved a lot but lost him because of what Mario did to her. And she feels she has just started to live now that she got away from Mario even though she spent almost twenty-five years with him.

Edgar is working in a light bulb factory, packing them into boxes. So now we have light bulbs whenever we want. He is going to bring a box of them to you when he goes back to the rancho for Christmas. He says that there will be work for Rogelio in the same factory, if he wants to come. I don't know how he will get here, it is more difficult now to cross. He will have to go to Los Angeles first and stay with our cousin Esther, then come over to Chicago.

About Edgar, we think he has a novia because every Saturday night and Sunday afternoon he dresses up in his best clothes and boots and sombrero and goes out with a smile but not telling us where. It took him a long time to get over Gabriela and I think he still feels badly for how Oníforo treats here. Did I ever tell you he bought her glasses before he left Los Angeles? In any case Edgar seems happier now that he is in Chicago and doesn't have to see Oníforo mistreating Gabriela. He has even learned to write his name though I think he is bitter because Papá didn't let him go to school because he was the oldest boy and Papá needed him to help with the milpa.

Miguelito will be starting in a new school next January, it is a few blocks away . I got my amnesty papers, Mamá, before I came to Chicago. Someone I worked for gave me a letter saying I had cleaned her house since 1981. She didn't want me to go, she said, my work was so good. I had the telephone bills in my name too. Edgar came before he arranged amnesty so he didn't get it, even though he has been here long enough. That's why he'll have to struggle again to cross the border. He didn't have any proofs of living in Los Angeles since the telephone bill was *in my name and the electric bill in Mundo's name, and the rent receipts in Antonio's name, and Edgar had changed jobs so often and didn't know how to get in touch with his patrones anyway. And he has only been a little over two years here in Chicago although Aunt Lidia has let him put the telephone in his name so he can prove that.*

I will not go back to Antonio, Mamá, he has not even called since I left. I know you told me not to marry him but I loved him so and he changed here in Los Angeles because of all the bars and vice centers that we don't have on the rancho, you have to go all the way to Fresnillo to find them, as you know. And here they all have cars and go wherever they want and put anyone in them they want and it took half a day on horseback to get to Fresnillo and no one had any money to go to the vice centers anyway, unless it was after harvest time and scarcely even then. And I was not going to live with his threatening to hit me all the time when I asked where he had been as you did with my Papá before we lost him. I am not being disrespectful, Mamá, but you put up with a lot that we don't have to here. And he was being mean to Miguelito, worse that Papá was with Edgar, and I began dreaming again and again about the time he hit Miguelito over the head with the beer bottle, not on purpose, he was trying to hit me, but in my dreams sometimes Miguelito lost consciousness and didn't wake up. I can work here, Mamá, and I know I gave my wedding vows but there was adultery and here even if a man goes with another woman it is adultery, which is true in my beloved Mexico as well but everyone lets the man get away with it. And women don't have to put up with it just so the children will eat and have clothes and shoes and school supplies. Because I can work and earn my little centavitos, Mamá. I will keep sending you something every two months, although it will be less at first than when I was in Los Angeles because here I absolutely must help Aunt Lidia pay the rent, which Edgar helps with also, as he did when he lived with us in Los Angeles. If Rogelio comes he will be able to help us out. Between us we will get the money to pay the coyote, even if we have to borrow some.

Please have my sister Berta write to me to tell me how you all are and don't take my decision about leaving Antonio badly Mamá. I don't want to live a life of hell, him after other women then threatening to hit me and my children, a life of misery like other women we have known Mamá. Miguelito and I will be all right here with my brother Edgar and my tía Lidia.

May the Virgin Mary protect you and my brother Rogelio and sister
Berta, as these are my desires.
Lucha

1990-1991

Fifteen: **1990**

By 1990 Lucy had returned, pregnant, to the *rancho* Santa Martha. She was accompanied by the 22-year-old father, who she met in Los Angeles, but who had come from a *rancho* only eighteen kilometers from the one where she was born. He had never found stable employment in Los Angeles. Mundo had assured him that he could use the *ejido* lands still in Mundo's name.

By 1990, Petra and Benjamin had joined Mundo in West Los Angeles. They eventually rented a row house in Venice, in a complex consisting of three side-by-side apartments fronting a small yard. Two were occupied by other families from Zacatecas.

Lucha, her brother Edgar, and a younger brother, Rogelio, who had joined them there, remained in Chicago.

Antonio spent most of his money in bars, often accompanied by his brother-in-law Oníforo.

Mundo, Antonio, Luís, Ignacio, Lucha, and Lucha's *tía* Lidia had received general amnesty. Nicolás and Ignacio had received Special Agricultural Workers amnesty.Edgar, Rogelio, Gabriela and Oníforo had not. Ignacio lost his residence card on a drinking spree in Salinas during the lettuce harvest one year. The *migra* refused to replace it. He continued to cross through the hole in Colonia Baja California for the lettuce harvest in the Imperial Valley, but did not take the bus north to Salinas.

Gabriela thought about returning to the *rancho*, where she would have at least the love of her mother to help her get through the days.

Sixteen: **Benjamin**

Petra was adding the *nopales* to the fried bits of pork when she heard the shooting. There were shootings off of guns at least twice a month. But this lasted longer. Not as long as the time they went to East L.A. to visit Ariseli and her husband on New Year's eve. But longer than the shootings at dances in Santa Anita or Santa Margarita. She had sent Benjamin to buy tortillas at the store two blocks away. She didn't like him to be outside when people were firing off guns. It was early for such gunfire. Usually it happened after sundown, when Mundo was home. More usually it happened after midnight, when the neighbors down the street got drunk or strung out on cocaine. She hoped Benjamin would not become a *grifo*, or use even harder drugs, as so many young Mexican-Americans. Chicanos they are called she reminded herself.

She rinsed her hands and walked drying them on the dishtowel she had bought last week at Woolworths in Santa Monica, to the door. The shooting had stopped, but there was a lot of shouting going on. She didn't understand about what, because it was in English. Hopefully Benjamin was still in the store or had run into his *tía* Gabriela's when the shooting started. She twisted the new green dishtowel in her hands. She walked through the muddy yard, to the dilapidated wooden gate. Should she look out? Mundo said women should not witness the shootings carried out by men. But he was not here, and she had sent Benjamin to the store. He would not be home for another half hour or so. And the shouts were receding.

She opened the sagging wooden gate and looked in the direction Benjamin had taken to the store. She began running, holding on to the dish towel crying "no, no" as she saw the crumpled body of her child, laying on the corner.

In the distance she saw Gabriela come out on the porch, her daughter held in her arms, and begin walking toward her.

Benjamin was lying in a pool of blood, gushing from his stomach. He was still twitching when she got to his side. She lifted his head to put the dish towel under it, so he would not dirty his hair in the dust of the street. And she sobbed, "no, no, not my little son. Not my Benjamin. Oh what will Mundo say. He will be so angry. My son, my only son. The only son I can ever have."

Gabriela reached her, touched her shoulder, as Benjamin convulsed one last time and died.

They held the first three days of the wake in their small house in Venice. The rest of the nine day *novena* would be held on the *rancho*. The *rancho* Santa Martha, where Benjamin was born and where he would be buried. Petra was glad that Mundo had decided, after much ruminating, not to hunt down the killer, though Oníforo and some of the boys in Apartment 25 urged him to do so. They didn't know who had shot the fatal bullet in any case, or even who was doing the shooting.

On the last day in July, Mundo and Petra and their five-year-old daughter Alicia accompanied Benjamin's coffin back to the *rancho* Santa Martha, first taking the plane to the city of Zacatecas, then hiring a car and driver for $100 to drive them to their destination. For six days they held a wake in Mundo's mother's house for their lost son. Everyone from the *rancho* and some people from nearby *ranchos* came to sit by the coffin and drink the cinnamon flavored coffee that Petra and his mother prepared. Every family on the *rancho* had someone in the United States, mostly in Los Angeles, and each family feared that something could happen to their loved ones, a fear made more real by Benjamin's little bullet-ridden body. Even the innocent, even a child, could meet a premature death on the other side.

After the 9th day, Mundo and his family made their way up to the *monte* and buried the small coffin near a *cordón*. The *monte*, where lovers met, and the dead were buried. They put up a white wooden cross, adorned with wildflowers, before they turned back and walked the two kilometers to the rancho.

Nicolás came back for the funeral from Salinas, stopping in Mexicali to collect Miranda and the children. Most of the family in Los Angeles would not attend. Ignacio had been on the *rancho* visiting his wife, so he was there.

Gabriela could not come because she feared crossing back *sin papeles*, and her seldom employed husband would have no money to pay for the *coyote* in any case, especially if she brought their son, who was also undocumented with her, unlike his little sister. And with whom could she leave the children? She was not quite ready to go back to the *rancho* yet. Lucy had gone back to the *rancho* more than a year ago to give birth to her daughter and stayed. Lucy's husband was farming Mundo's two hectares and her two brothers sent her money occasionally, as did Gabriela. Lucha was in Chicago, and Petra had left with her dead son.

Antonio had given Mundo some money for his and Petra's return trip to the *rancho*, but felt he could not leave his gardening route, even for a few days. While Mundo understood Gabriela's quandary, he found Antonio's absence almost unforgiveable. Antonio, after all, had his residence permit and could cross back and forth easily. It just added to the strain Mundo felt after Antonio hit Miguelito with the beer bottle—even though it was an accident. He had been trying to hit Lucha.

Petra had let it be known that she would never return to their house in Venice, or anywhere else in Los Angeles, or in the United States. Mundo pointed out that he could not support them just by working his two hectares of cornfields. That he would have to return to Los Angeles, that he could not stay. But now that he had his papers he could return every year or even every six months. There would be no *coyote* fees to pay, no dangerous crossings, no need to wait two years or more to return to the *rancho*. Now there need not be such a long separation, he had documents, and yes, it was better that she stayed back on the *rancho* with their daughter—far away from the gangs whose stray bullets had mowed down their son. His mother, whose tears had lasted for weeks, had convinced him of this with little effort. He would never have another son, at least not with Petra. She had injured herself giving birth to Alicia, and the doctor they had had to see, told her that she could no longer get pregnant.

When more than a month of grieving had past and it came time for him to go back to Los Angeles to earn some much needed money, Mundo was still disoriented from the loss of his beloved and only son. But he decided not to take the long route back to Tecate or Tijuana where previously he and his brother and his cousin Luís had crossed *de mojado*. That had meant taking the bus from Fresnillo to Guadalajara and then catching another bus for the 38-hour trip to the border, though Jalisco, Nayarit, Sinaloa and Sonora until reaching Baja California. This time he would cross in El Paso, catching the bus from Fresnillo to Cuidad Juárez and then take the Golden State bus from El Paso to Los Angeles, with no fear of immigration checkpoints along the way. He had never crossed alone before, but it should be easy now that he had his residence card.

One early morning in August Mundo found a ride to Fresnillo and then caught an Estrella Blanca bus for Cuidad Juárez. He was surprised to see a man about his age who had crossed with the same *coyote* from Tecate in 1984 sitting alone in the back of the bus. Mundo didn't remember his name but he did remember that he was from Guanajuato, that he lived in East Los Angeles and had worked in construction. Mundo tipped his *tejana* to him, and the man motioned for him to sit down in the empty seat beside him. Mundo sat, then reached over, offered his hand, and said "Mundo Contreras, *para servirle*."

The man replied, "Alejandro Cabello, *para servirle*." Then Mundo asked him if he remembered crossing from Tecate more than seven years ago.

"Yes, of course," said Alejandro. "I recognized you. Where are you going?"

"Back to Los Angeles," replied Mundo, "but this time with papers."

"Me, too," said Alejandro.

"You going back to Los Angeles too?" Mundo asked.

"No, actually I am going to Walton, Georgia," said Alejandro.

"Working in construction?" asked Mundo, remembering Alejandro years before had told him that he worked in construction cleanup.

"No, you never know when there will be work in construction. Months on, months off. I'm working steady on a chicken farm."

The concept of a chicken farm was new to Mundo. Almost everyone on the *rancho* had chickens, at least two or three, and often a dozen or so, but a "farm" implied lots of chickens. "How many chickens are there on the farm?" he asked Alejandro.

"About 3,000, sometimes more. About 1,000 are laying hens and the others are capons for eating."

Mundo thought for awhile, about such an immense number of chickens. "Who buys that many chickens and that many eggs?" he asked.

"Mostly the supermarkets. The boss makes a contract with a supermarket chain and they buy everything up."

"How did you find that job? How far away is the farm from Los Angeles?" Mundo asked.

Alejandro answered the last question first. "Well, it's about a thousand miles or more from El Paso to Los Angeles and it's almost a thousand more in the other direction to Atlanta, Georgia."

Mundo mulled over these great distances and then asked, "How did you ever land there?"

"Well, a *compadre* of mine was recruited there some years ago. A contractor came by the church where he lived in East Los Angeles and asked for twenty men, free transport, $40 a day, could bring their families. My *compadre* didn't have a family anymore, and he wanted to get out of Los Angeles, or any big city, so he volunteered to go. Then later he called me up and asked me to join him."

"He didn't have any family?" Mundo asked, wondering how he could have come across the border without brothers and cousins and an uncle to join.

"No, his wife died giving birth to their first child before he came across. He didn't have money to pay for a doctor or put her in a clinic, so she died. The baby died too. He never got over it. And before that his brother and his mother and father died in a bus crash outside of Guadalajara, coming back from visiting his mother's sister. He only had one brother. He has had it hard."

Mundo started turning his *tejana* around in this hands, brushing the brim with his fingers. Maybe someday he would tell Alejandro of his own sadness. "So you joined your *compadre* in Georgia?"

"You got it," said Alejandro, "and it's the best thing I did. The pay is good. Double for overtime. There are no gangs around. Almost no crime. Except for someone stealing a chicken that wanders off the grounds," he said, looking at Mundo and almost smiling.

"How many workers have they got?" Mundo asked.

"About 100, an average of one for every 300 chickens. And then there are another 2,000 chicks or so that I forgot to mention. So one for every 500 chickens. Why, are you thinking of working there? I can tell the boss next time we have an opening. Or just come out with me now. There are a lot of other chicken farms nearby."

Mundo looked sidewise at Alejandro. "Let me think about it." And as the sky darkened and the passengers settled back in their seats that evening, he thought about it.

His cousin Nicolás and *tío* Ignacio were no longer in Los Angeles. They worked in the lettuce fields in the Imperial Valley and Nicolás followed the harvest to Salinas. His relationship with his brother

Antonio had been strained since the incident with Miguelito that led Lucha to leaving him. And then he had not even come back to the *rancho* for the funeral. Antonio could find someone to replace him permanently on Sawtelle, as he did temporarily when Mundo was gone. Or maybe Luís would like the job. In any case, Los Angeles held bad memories. Would he ever be able to walk around Venice or Santa Monica or West Los Angeles, or go to the Santa Monica Pier where they had taken Benjamin almost every Sunday, without remembering the fragile body of his eleven year old son resting in a pool of blood? Would such thoughts drive him to drunkenness or even make him lose his mind?

And further, chicken farming might be good to learn. Maybe he could get to know how to farm chickens, whatever that entailed, and be able to go back to the *rancho* and farm chickens on at least one of this two hectares, and use the other to grow corn for feed for them and tortillas for his family. Then he would be able to be with Petra and Alicia and his mother and his little brother and sister. Maybe just start with a few hundred. He could get his little brother to work for him. There were markets in Fresnillo and in the city of Zacatecas that he could sell to.

As the morning dawned, as they came into the dusty outskirts of Cuidad Juárez, Mundo turned to Alejandro and with a small smile said, "Thank you for your offer. With great pleasure I will come to Georgia with you."

About the Author

Tamar Diana Wilson combined poetry, creative non-fiction, and academic chapters in her *Subsidizing Capitalism: Brickmakers on the U.S.-Mexico Border* (Albany: SUNY Press, 2005). Her creative non-fiction collection *Tales from Colonia Popular* (Austin: Plain View Press) was published in 2009 as was her non-fiction *Women's Migration Networks in Mexico and Beyond* (Albuquerque: University of New Mexico Press). She has published articles on immigration, the informal sector, and gender issues in *Anthropological Quarterly*, *Critique of Anthropology*, *Journal of Borderlands Studies*, *Human Organization*, *Latin American Perspectives*, *Review of Radical Political Economics*, *Violence Against Women, and Urban Anthropology*. Her fiction and poetry have appeared in *Struggle, Anthropology & Humanism, Saturday Night Journal, Thema, Blue Mesa Review* and in two collections of poetry, one edited by Terry Wolverton and one by Candace Catlin Hall. She has lived in Mexico since 1988.

On top of my roof, Colonia Popular, Mexicali, 1989

9 781935 514367